THE TAMING OF VIOLET

MASIELLO BROTHERS BOOK 1

J.M. DABNEY

HOSTILE WHISPERS PRESS, LLC

To my readers who embrace all my voices.

CONTENTS

PREFACE

This is the first book in a series of 6 books. Each book is a stand-alone titles as it's a mixed pairings series. The series will include F/M (Female/Male), M/M (Male/Male), M/GF (Male/Gender-fluid), as well as a M/FTrans (Male/Female Transgender). These books will be able to read in any order and easily able to skip without feeling as if the read is missing anything.

PROLOGUE

"You punch like a fucking girl, Clem," Violet Canne taunted from her position on the ground. She took the stomps and the kicks with a smile on her face.

"I'll show you a girl, Violet."

The menace in her oldest brother's voice should've scared her. He snarled and brought the sole of his steel-toed boot down on her ribs harder. The pain was instant as she felt the bones give, but Violet didn't cry or even acknowledge it.

Seventeen years of beatings in the name of toughening her up taught her a valuable lesson. Weakness and pain were useless, they only invited more punishments—more lessons. This current round due to the university acceptance letter with a full academic ride she'd received. Violet hadn't gotten to the mailbox quicker than her brothers or father. It pristine envelop already sullied by their dirty grease-stained hands.

She's worked her ass off for that full scholarship. She wanted out of this fucking town and the endless series of shacks and motels that rotated every few months when either the money ran out or the current landlord lost their patience.

Peeking through her brother's legs and saw her father reading

1

the paper, folding the corner back every so often to check that the boys were doing their job. Clem, Garth, Chuck, and Lonnie were all older, but sure as fuck not meaner than her. She was female and the youngest, Alpha position was determined by who inflicted the most pain—wounds. Violet made sure she wasn't on the bottom often.

She was done letting them have their fun. She reached into the pocket of her pink dress and slipped her tiny hand into the brass knuckles. The agony and the flavored of blood on her tongue receded until nothing remained but the rage.

They considered her weaker, the runt of the litter, and she'd fought for survival—her place—since she three years old. She curled her body as if to protect herself, but quickly she attacked. She moved to her knees, upper cuts and wild swings forced her brothers back. Once on her feet, she didn't allow them to circle her. If she'd learned anything, never give these fuckers her back. She'd awakened too many times from being choked out and earning her father's disappointment and scorn.

She fought, giving as good as she got, but four, sometimes, five against one weren't odds in her favor.

An hour later, she slumped on a gurney in the emergency room while her father told the lie he always did. They lived in a bad neighborhood and she'd gotten jumped on the way home. The cops didn't give a fuck about some poor kid in a bad area. She wasn't a stranger to dealing with the police, most of them knew her name and record. Shit happened, they didn't want to waste time on the paperwork. It wasn't like she was going to talk anyway.

She'd lost track of what was in her medical file. The one that grew thicker every week. If she'd grown up normal she'd have seen it for what it was—abuse. Unfortunately, it was just her way of life and she survived by any means necessary. No one gave a shit about her and she knew it, her only chance was to get out of this town and never look back.

That's what she had college for and as much of a lost cause as everyone believed her to be she'd worked harder than everyone. They didn't have as much to lose as she did. She'd die if she didn't escape, either her brothers' beatings would go too far or some asshole on the street would punch her ticket. Violet didn't much care about dying. To her if it happened then it would be an escape. Just a lot more permanent than her plan A which was school and a new life. All of it would follow her, memories and scars telling a story as clearly as if they were inked marks on paper.

She simply needed to survive a bit longer—be stronger than the five men who shared DNA and spilled her blood in the name of making her better and tougher. She lived with her rage that permeated each cell—deep in her badly healed bones. Either they'd kill her or she'd kill them, but in the end she'd learn who possessed the most brutality. She was a product of her environment and she'd make sure failure wasn't her option.

HE WAS GOING TO KILL HER

*G*iovanni Masiello hugged the pillow to his ears. The death metal and screaming coming from the other side of the duplex he rented vibrated the wall behind his headboard. An hour of listening to it was driving him crazy and he needed to be awake at five a.m. to get to work. He jerked as a door slammed and he surged from his bed, wearing nothing but his boxers he ran to his front door and threw it open. He didn't give a fuck if he looked like a crazy man, he'd had enough of her shit.

Violet Canne was a pain in the ass.

The only reason he knew her name was because some of her mail was delivered to him a few days after she'd moved in a year ago. Instead of dealing with her he'd just shoved it into her mailbox. As far as he was concerned he'd never had to meet her. He couldn't do his job with no sleep.

There she was, dragging her trash can to the curb and he could hear her cursing from here. For all her cute looks, she was a hateful little woman. Every date he'd had over the last year since she moved in was ruined by death metal or loud noises through the wall. Who the hell could keep it up with the men's guttural screams that his neighbor considered music blaring at all hours?

He stormed off the small stoop.

"Could you turn down your fucking music, woman, some people actually sleep in this neighborhood."

She slowed panned until she stared at him. "What you call me?"

"Woman, so turn down the music so I can work in the goddamn morning."

His eyes widened at her sudden growl, the way her big eyes rounded even more and he barely had time to realize what was happening before she was running at him. A tiny shoulder connected with his abdomen. In shock he found his back hitting the dewy grass and the air was driven out of his lungs.

"I'll show you woman, you overgrown man child."

Tiny fists started to pummel him and just as he went to grab her wrists, the beam of a flashlight blinded him.

"Freeze, police, ma'am, I suggest—"

It was like she didn't know a cop stood behind her with his gun drawn. Hell, the crazy woman might not even care. He sat up so fast to try and calm the situation that his nose collided with her forehead, his vision danced at the pain. "Fuck," he cursed. He raised his hand to finger the bridge of his nose.

She fought the cop as she was grabbed around the waist and pulled off him.

"I'm going to ki—"

"Violet!" His voice harsher than he'd ever heard it. He was the even tempered one of his brothers. He never got angry or frustrated. He was always the referee between his brothers and there were seven of them so he played the role of peacekeeper a lot.

Her gaze locked on him and he knew the moment realization dawned, her eyes widened and her bottom lip started trembling. He felt a moment of remorse at her confusion.

"Why am I outside?"

He didn't know how to answer that, but he didn't have a chance when he realized she was being cuffed, read her rights. At least he recognized the cops from his job.

"Man, come on, she was just sleepwalking or something. She didn't even know she was outside." He didn't know why he was trying to protect her, maybe it was the teary eyes and the wobbly lush bottom lip. His parents drilled into him and his brothers from an early age to always be a gentleman and the lessons stuck. Even if Violet seemed impossible and a bit off in the head, he couldn't let her get locked up.

"Sorry, we witnessed—"

"I'm not pressing charges. Just let her go, I'll take her into her place and make sure she's all settled."

"You sure, Gio, she looks dangerous."

"She's five foot nothing, how dangerous could she be?"

He almost had the urge to laugh as she started kicking at him and swung her tiny fists. This was not the time to be amused.

"You bastard, I'll show you—"

"Violet!" He yelled to get her attention again. The woman was going to get her curvy ass arrested.

Luckily, they removed the cuffs and stepped back as she rubbed her wrists. He could already tell she had no respect for authority because she glared at the cops just as much as she had done him.

"Lady, you better be glad Gio here is understanding or you'd spend your night in jail."

He watched her open her mouth and he cut her off. "I'm sure she's very appreciative." He reached down and she was so short, he could only reach her ribs. He steered Violet toward her house. His fingers and thumb sunk into the soft flesh of her sides.

Once he had her inside, he kicked the door closed and went to turn the music off. He jerked as he noticed the heavy bag hanging in the middle of her empty living room. As far as he could see she had no furniture in any of the rooms. No pictures hung on her walls or were tucked into the built in shelves of the living room.

He pressed the power button on her wireless speakers and pivoted to find her warily watching him. The house was blessedly quiet. Her fists clenched and relaxed at her sides as she seemed to take deep even breaths then exhaled slowly.

She was cute even if a little psychotic.

That's when he noticed the remnants of a shattered cell phone scattered across the hardwood floor.

"Bad day?"

"Every day is bad."

"What made today bad," He surprised himself when he asked. He had to be up in four hours. He was a firefighter, he didn't have the luxury of going to work exhausted. It wasn't safe for him or the men he worked with—considered family.

Violet took a deep breath in and exhaled slowly, "Well, my day started with me imagining plucking the eyes out of the Bridezilla who thinks she can have every crazy idea come true."

Wow, he hadn't exactly seen the woman as a wedding planner. He'd always assumed someone with that kind of job would need to be positive and bubbly.

"Normally, brides want their big day to be special."

"She wants everything in gold, every thing. If I have to look at another cherub I'm going to take a baseball bat to those chubby fuckers."

The corners of his mouth started to twitch and she let out another cute little growl. "What else?"

"Another bride's mother wants me to have the bride's wedding dress made two sizes too small to shame her size eight daughter into losing weight. Fuck, forbid someone have some hips. The bride barely has tits and there's not enough stuffing in the world to fill in the bust of her dress."

"Keep going."

"My new boyfriend said that he wouldn't fuck me because he

said my ass jiggling turned him off. Is my ass too fat," Violet asked and spun, pulling up the back of her flowery dress.

He nearly swallowed his tongue as the cutest dimpled ass cheeks he'd ever seen were exposed by her raised dress and plain white boy shorts.

That was an ass a man spanked when he had her bent over the nearest surface. Violet had the kind of curves that only a real man could appreciate. What the fuck was he thinking?

"Well?"

He realized he'd been staring too long. "There is absolutely nothing fat about your ass."

She grabbed her ass cheeks in her hands and gave the plump curves a little shake.

He wondered what she'd say if he asked her to bend over and spread them for him. Boxers weren't the attire to wear for the thoughts he was having about her lush curves. His gaze moved down to rounded thighs with no gap in sight.

Less than an hour ago he'd contemplated killing her and now he had the uncontrollable urge to fuck her. That wasn't happening. He was delirious from lack of sleep or he was still in his bed having a nightmare. He hoped it was a fucking nightmare.

"I'm a size twenty, of course I'm fat," She rolled her eyes as she glanced at him over her shoulder and then let her dress fall.

He almost ordered her to lift her skirt again so he could fall to his knees and worship her ass the way it deserved. He scrubbed his hands over his face.

"I need a drink," she announced and rushed in the direction of the kitchen.

Violet and alcohol terrified him, he jogged after her to talk her out of getting drunk. He'd had all he could take for one night. He froze in the doorway of her kitchen to find her with a half-gallon of chocolate milk turned up. He had the urge to throw his hands in the air and scream why as he watched her chugging with her hand up the back of her dress working the clasp of her bra loose.

Did she not realize she had some strange man in her house? Sane women wouldn't lift their skirts and ask him was their ass fat. They sure as hell wouldn't be working to remove their bra.

She put the cap back on the carton and shoved it into the fridge and as if she were performing a magic trick she removed her bra. The sigh that passed her full lips had his—no, this wasn't happening. The bra sailed through the air and landed on the counter next to him. It was all red silk and lace, to be honest he hadn't seen that much material in a bra in his life.

She kicked the fridge door shut and he jerked his gaze back to her to find her rubbing her breasts. She let out the sexiest moan he'd heard in his life.

"I've gotta go, I have work in the morning."

He turned without waiting for a goodbye and it was only his pride that kept him from running away as if his fuzzy ass was on fire. Who the fuck had he pissed off in a past life to warrant this amount of torture?? His crazy neighbor had him hard in no time from just a peek of her ass and then she had to rub the massive curves of her breasts. The bad thing was it was done in the most unsexy way and that had still turned him on. He didn't breathe easy until he was locked inside his place. He needed to get laid and soon, because if his psycho neighbor got his dick hard he needed help.

SHE THOUGHT SHE'D DO WELL IN PRISON

*V*iolet stroked her thumb across the screen of her new phone. This was her fourth one in two years and she tried to hit a different store every time she needed to replace it. When she was a kid, flip phones were indestructible, but the new ones, one good throw against a wall and she needed a brand new one.

She felt calmer after her rage rub before she dragged herself out of bed. A good orgasm always cleared her head. She mentally made a note: she needed new batteries. She'd get those after her anger management group later that evening, after that she'd have to apologize to her neighbor.

Other people wouldn't be so understanding about being tackled by her in the middle of the night. Although she thought she'd do well in prison.

Maybe she could apologize early, she'd seen the station number on his uniform for the firehouse he worked at. Men liked sweets. Or she thought they did. She didn't have much experience with what men liked or didn't like. The only thing she knew for sure was they didn't like her too much.

She ducked into a bakery and stood at the counter, a bubbly

woman behind the counter had her snarling her nose and she squeezed her hand around her new phone.

Don't do it, Violet, don't do it, she repeated in her head.

Okay, she'd grown up in a home where happiness was frowned upon unless it was after a violent victory. She could take her four brothers down to the ground by the time she was eight. They counted their wins in stitches and black eyes. Her dad didn't look at her any different than her brothers. Thankfully her juvenile record was expunged on her eighteenth birthday. The real world had been a pain in the ass. She'd learned to handle her problems with fists or a baseball bat. Being a grownup she had to learn diplomacy—that shit wasn't her strong suit. Adjusting to a world where violence wasn't a daily occurrence had turned into the hardest lesson to learn.

At twenty-five she'd worked her way up in the event planning company she'd hired on with after college. She had her own clients and people asked for her by name. It should be something to take pride in, but even though she kept her temper in check during business hours she couldn't say the same for the rest of the time.

"Good afternoon, ma'am, what can I get for you today? Would you like to try anything?"

The vision of ruining that bright, perky smile brought a smile to her own lips.

"Actually, I need three dozen of whatever. I'm taking them to a firehouse."

"I'll get that together for you."

She felt herself move forward to jerk that bouncing ponytail and snatch the bitch bald. She closed her eyes and worked to slow her breathing and bring her irritation levels down. Her shrink told her that it would take a while to work through the damage done by her childhood. Most days she didn't think anything was wrong with her, but last night proved she had a problem. She'd tackled a strange man and pummeled him, she barely remembered coming out of her house.

Thankfully, the donuts and pastries were boxed, paid for and she was out the door. She called a cab and when it arrived she gave the address. It wasn't too far from her office so she could walk back. She hoisted her messenger bag onto her shoulder. Checked her pale pink dress and scuffed the toes of her Mary Jane's on the backs of her calves.

She knew the man's name because the cop called him Gio. Maybe he wouldn't be there and she wouldn't have to pretend to be nice. She walked toward the bay and froze at a huge dark-haired man with a blue t-shirt straining across his back muscles and an ass that screamed for her to spank or bite. She closed her eyes again and took deep breaths.

Once she was calm she stepped forward.

"Ma'am, can I help you," another huge guy asked.

Was it the land of giants around this fucking place?

"I'm looking for Gio."

She didn't know why the guy suddenly had a huge grin on his face, but she wanted to punch—*Violet, calm down.*

"Right this way, Bro, you got a visitor."

The big man with the ass she'd just been ogling turned around. He was so handsome she wanted to mess up his face. Mere mortals shouldn't be that fucking gorgeous or sexy.

"Violet, what are you doing here?"

She inhaled deeply, "I wanted to say I'm sorry for tackling you last night and thanks for not letting me be arrested. Although, I think I'd do well in prison." She thrust the three massive boxes in his direction and forced him to take them.

"Oh, you didn't have to apologize, you were having—"

"Just take the fucking donuts," she hissed under her breath.

The giant that was Gio's brother started to laugh and she snarled her nose.

"Violet!"

She clenched her back teeth and unclenched her fists she hadn't even noticed she'd curled. Then she noticed Gio's brother was looking at Gio with a strange look on his face.

"You shouldn't use that tone with her, Gio."

"Renz, take a walk,," Gio ordered.

"I'm just saying. You should treat her with more respect. Just wait until I tell Ma, she's going to be so disappointed in you."

She studied Renz and wondered where the hell these people came from. Also, what kind of name was Renz?

"Take these to the break room."

"I should go, my lunch is almost over. Um, I'll keep my music down. I got new earbuds today."

"Do you think that's wise, you'll ruin your hearing."

"I'll be fine. I don't know what's in the boxes, I just told them to put whatever in." She started to turn.

"Violet, thanks."

"You're welcome."

"You look very pretty today."

She felt her brows pull together and her lips tug into a frown. Should firemen drink or do drugs on duty?

"What?"

"Just saying."

"Thanks, I guess. I've gotta go."

Her cheeks felt funny like they were on fire. Almost like when she got pissed, but she wasn't feeling angry. No one ever called her pretty before. She dug her phone from her bag and dialed her best friend.

Her friend's sweet voice said hi and she ignored the pleasantries.

"Someone told me I was pretty and my face felt funny, like it was burning."

"Violet, that's called a blush. Normal women do that when given a compliment."

"Why was I given a compliment? Have you seen me? I'm a

train wreck of rolls and stretch marks, don't even get me started on dimples."

"You're being paranoid, we've talked about this. You're a very beautiful woman."

"The newest boyfriend—"

"You dated him for two months. He wouldn't even take you to meet his parents."

"He wouldn't fuck me either. Said my ass jiggled too much."

She didn't care about things like that. Sure, she was a little insecure about parts of her, but really, she boxed and she walked everywhere she went. So, it wasn't like she didn't get exercise. For as long as she could remember she'd been chunky and she was okay with it. If men didn't like it, so what, her toys got her off just fine.

"There is absolutely nothing wrong with your ass."

"Why do people talk about their flesh suits like they're something to be proud of?"

"We're not going to get into this again."

"But, Lauren, it's squiggy skin slapped over the internal ugly bits. Why do they put so much importance on—oh fuck!"

"What," Lauren yelled.

"I showed some strange man my ass last night, lifted my dress and asked him if my ass was too fat."

Lauren giggled, "You need supervision."

"Celibate is the way to go, that's worked for me."

"Um, I think as much as you masturbate and the fortune you spend in batteries, you're not celibate."

"A girl has needs and no man wants to take care of mine. We do what we gotta do."

"Men aren't all they're cracked up to be, Violet."

Lauren sounded sad. "How's the fetus?"

"Your goddaughter is fine."

"You haven't had an ultrasound yet, how do you know it's a girl?"

"I just have a feeling."

Lauren had found out she was pregnant a month before and her boyfriend had been out the door the next day. The bastard hadn't even bothered to say goodbye. He'd just left a note on the kitchen table. It wasn't like the bastard went very far. Lauren had to see the man every day at work. That why people shouldn't buy their meat where they make their bread, too much weirdness when shit fell apart.

"Dinner at my place tonight?"

"That would be great, I need out of the house. I go to work and come home, it's getting boring."

"Be at my place at five and we'll order in."

"Of course we'll order in, but don't you have your meeting tonight?"

"I can skip one. It's no big deal."

They weren't court ordered so it wasn't like she was going to get in trouble if she skipped one. She could go to two meetings next week.

"When are you going to buy furniture and actually put groceries in your fridge?"

"One day, I promise."

"You keep saying one day and it's been a year, you still haven't done it."

"I'm fine. People put too much stock in material shit. I got what I need." She didn't want to argue about this shit and it always turned into a pissing contest with Lauren trying to convince her she needed to settle in and start living a normal life. She didn't know shit about being normal.

They said their goodbyes as she reached her office. So, what was the big deal, she hadn't settled into her place yet. A year ago she was Lauren's roommate before Lauren got serious with her boyfriend and Violet thought they'd need some privacy. She couldn't bring herself to make that house a home. Her dad and brothers were always in trouble and they'd moved a lot. She'd lived out of suitcases and motel rooms for most of her teens.

She just didn't understand normal. She watched all those people going about their lives so content. The couples so happy together. She didn't understand and she knew she never would, she knew how to survive; no one ever taught her anything else.

SHE WAS ACTUALLY SWEET UNDER
THAT PSYCHOTIC EXTERIOR

*G*io stood at his kitchen window and stared out at their shared backyard. He had the window up and he could hear Violet and another woman talking, or more exactly Violet was laying on her stomach and talking to the woman's belly. Violet was sweet, he hadn't expected that. He smiled when he remembered her blush when he told her she was pretty after she'd stopped by with the bakery boxes. He wondered if no one had ever said that to her before.

Rude or not, he listened in on the conversation.

"Violet, she can't hear you yet."

He heard the amusement in the strange woman's voice.

"Let me do this, okay, now, since you're my goddaughter and you will be called Gina."

"Why Gina?"

He leaned heavier on the sink and pressed his face closer to the screen. Part of him wanted to go outside just so he could possibly spend more time with the woman. He'd spent the last week not being able to think about anything but Violet, her curves and her hatefulness. That shit shouldn't turn him on, but there was something about Violet that he couldn't seem to resist.

"Because it's my middle name and I say so."

"Why are we friends again?"

"Because no one else wants to put up with me, now, hush. So, Gina," Violet rubbed her chin on her friend's exposed belly, "The greatest lesson to learn in life is how to throw a proper punch."

He snorted and instantly covered his mouth. He didn't need to be caught, but Violet wanting to teach an unborn baby how to throw a punch was just too Violet.

"Violet, you're not teaching my daughter how to throw the perfect punch before she'd escaped the uterine prison."

"These are important lessons to learn. Do you know how many black eyes and busted lips I avoided growing up? Dude, I could've been a heavyweight."

He frowned at the thought someone would put their hands on the tiny woman. Yes, she was plus-sized, but she was still a woman even with her anger issues. If she'd grown up in an abusive home then she didn't know any better. From what it sounded like she had.

"We've talked about this."

"We talk about a lot of things. Will I squish the fetus?"

"No you won't squish her."

He leaned closer to the window his nose almost touched the screen as Violet turned over and laid her head on her friend's stomach. The woman combed her fingers through Violet's hair.

"Have you talked to your dad and brothers recently?"

"I called dad at rehab a few weeks ago. Did visiting hours with the sibs except for Clem. I haven't had time to drive to Kentucky yet."

"When are they up for parole?"

"Staggered over the next year or two, they talked about coming here to stay."

"Violet, that's not a good idea. The last time you all lived together what happened?"

"It wasn't all bad, Lauren."

"It definitely wasn't all good. You're still living in the past. No furniture in your house. You won't even buy groceries. The only things you own are a punching bag and a bed."

"Don't forget my toys."

"Okay, your pleasure chest goes everywhere with you. There's this nice guy who just started at work."

He frowned at Lauren's attempt at a set up and he didn't want anyone near Violet. It might not be the sanest decision he'd ever made, but he wanted to get to know the woman—bad attitude and all.

"No, I don't want blind dates. If I was normal—"

"You are normal, just your own brand of it. Your dad made you and your brothers brawl for hierarchy, he didn't care if you were the baby and a girl."

"Mom wasn't any better it wasn't just dad."

"Your mom's a pit boss in Vegas."

"We all have our talents."

"They considered you the runt of the pack and needed to—"

"Lauren, life isn't all roses and happiness. Some of us just take what we can get. Do you want to order food now?"

He had an idea. He stepped out of the door off the kitchen and descended the steps, both women turned his way. He almost smiled at the way Violet sat up, then smoothed Lauren's shirt back over her soft belly. Her touch lingering a bit. The woman wasn't all psychotic tendencies.

"Hello, Violet."

"Gio, um, this is my friend, Lauren."

"Nice to meet you, what are y'all doing?"

"Violet was just going to work her impressive skills and order us takeout."

"I was about to heat up the grill. Why don't you two join me? Eating alone sucks." He didn't mention that he never had to eat alone. His brothers were getting together at their favorite pub for dinner. He'd planned to go, but he couldn't get passed the urge he had to spend time with the crazy, little woman. He didn't know what happened to him since he'd met Violet.

"We wouldn't want to be a bother."

Lauren was sweet, all light and happiness while Violet was Violet. He studied Lauren for a minute, she had curves that matched Violet's, but a few inches taller. Although, nothing about Lauren got his cock perking up like just a thought of Violet had done.

"It wouldn't be a bother. I come from a family of eight kids. Even living on my own for the last twenty years I still miss the chaos."

"I can't offer anything," Violet said as she got to her feet and started to help Lauren up.

"Violet, I'm two months pregnant, I'm perfectly capable of getting up on my own."

"Shut up and let me help, fuck, do as I say."

He covered his smile with his hand as the two women argued and Violet didn't let her friend go until she made sure Lauren was steady on her feet. That was weird after he knew she could tackle a grown man to the ground with no fear. He didn't expect her to be kind and attentive, but she was doing it for her best friend who was pregnant. That had to be different.

"You don't have to offer anything. It's just steaks, but if y'all want to help that would be great. I was going to roast some potatoes and veggies."

"We can do that."

Lauren made the offer while Violet seemed to turn quiet and withdrawn.

"Come on to the house." He turned and headed back to his side of the yard.

"When did the massive hottie move in next door and why wasn't I told," Lauren's whisper wasn't quiet enough and he suppressed a chuckle.

"He lived here first."

He liked that she didn't deny the hottie remark. He wasn't vain. In his family actions dictated were what people were judged on, whether they were kind and respectful. Not that him and his brothers didn't know they were attractive and the fact they were firefighters got them a good amount of attention. All of that proved they weren't ogres.

He opened the door and motioned them inside first, Violet's ample ass right in his face as she passed him on the steps. He'd dreamed of those curves last night and wondered what it would feel like to wake up with them pushing back against his dick. He did love slow, lazy morning sex. He'd been single too long and it was seriously fucking with his head.

"You know where everything is, the places are mirror images of each other. Help yourself to whatever is in the fridge. I have a few beers, but I'm not much of a drinker."

"I don't drink." Violet said as she opened the fridge and pulled out a bottle of water for Lauren. "You don't have chocolate milk." She handed the bottle to Lauren. "I'll be right back." Violet left the kitchen through the back door.

"You've committed a mortal sin," Lauren whispered as she slightly leaned into his side.

He had a sense that it wasn't her flirting just the way she was, so he relaxed. The angelic blonde just wasn't his type, hell, until last night he hadn't considered Violet his type either.

"What's with her and chocolate milk?"

"I don't know, but when we met in college you never saw her without a half gallon."

He didn't think Lauren was telling the entire truth but he wasn't going to push. He'd like to discover some of Violet's secrets on his own. From her actions he didn't think Violet looked at him like a man. She'd lifted her dress without problem and asked was her ass fat. She removed her bra and threw it across the room, then massaged her tits right in front of him. It kind of stung his pride that she didn't seem attracted to him.

"Let's get started on the veggies, those are going to take a bit on the grill."

The back door opened just as he was pulling stuff out of the fridge, she came in with two half gallon cartons of chocolate milk. The side of her breast stroked across his cheek as she shoved the cartons onto the top shelf. Why the fuck was the woman's every move and action an instant hard-on and she was immune to him? It wasn't fair.

Lauren and him kept up a steady stream of conversation but Violet remained quiet as she slowly sliced the potatoes thin as they filled three foil packets to go on the grill. He had everything ready, veggies on the grill and steaks ready to go.

Lauren was sweet and funny, but Violet seemed more with-drawn as the night went on and he wanted to ask what was wrong. Lauren tried to draw her into conversation, her answers were short. She seemed to be leaving him and Lauren alone, then it hit him. She was leaving the conversation open for him and her friend.

"Better day today, Violet?"

"I thought about snatching the bakery girl bald and I didn't do it. Improvement."

He smiled as she tensed at what she said. The woman didn't know how to behave or what not to say, it was kind of nice in a strange way. He also realized something else, Violet really didn't see herself as a desirable woman. He didn't even know if she saw herself as a woman.

"The stuff you brought by the house today didn't last long. The guys cleared everything out as quick as they could."

"You got some right?"

"Yeah, that's only after I tackled my brothers Renz and Niccolo to get to the boxes."

"Survival of the fittest."

He had a feeling that was the motto for her life.

"Do you have a girlfriend, Gio?"

He turned to Lauren to find her smiling sweetly and her wink almost made him snort. Violet may be blind, but Lauren wasn't. Maybe he could have a secret weapon.

"No, not for a long time. Ma is a bit meddlesome when it comes to getting her boys paired off. She wants to make sure we're all partnered up and as happy as she is with our dad. For now, my oldest brother is the only one to get lucky and find his partner."

"Are you all firefighters?"

"Family tradition. I don't think any of us really considered being anything else. Most of us went to college, but afterward came home to apply. Job ain't the safest, hours suck most of the time, but for me it's what I always wanted to do. What do you do?"

"Personal assistant to the asshole CEO of an investment firm. Pays the bills, but not what I always wanted to do."

"What about you? I assume you're a wedding coordinator."

"It's an event planning company, we do everything from weddings to charity events. I needed a job after college, they were hiring and I seemed to be good at it."

"She's the best, everyone wants Violet Canne to plan their events. There isn't anything she can't make happen."

He could see the pride Lauren had in her friend. It was nice that Violet wasn't alone. "Time to throw the steaks on." He stood as he asked the ladies how they liked their steaks done.

The evening was a little more relaxed as they enjoyed dinner and when it was time for Lauren to go home, he wanted to ask them to stay longer. He knew as soon as Lauren was gone Violet would rush back to her house. He wanted to spend some time alone with Violet. See if he could win her over a bit, but he didn't see interest in her eyes when she looked at him. She didn't flirt or try to touch him.

Even though the skirts of her dresses were short she tended to dress a bit on the demure side. Nothing low cut or tight, but after seeing the red silk and lace bra, he wondered what she hid under her dresses. Most of the women he dated had matching bras and panties, he remembered the white cotton boy shorts paired with a sexy bra. He really had to stop thinking about her bras and panties because they made him think of dimpled cheeks he wanted to get his hands on and breasts he wanted to bury his face between.

He said bye to Lauren and accepted a thank you hug for dinner and Violet just said thank you as she led her friend back to her place. He walked back inside and frowned at the knock on the door. Most people who knew him called before they stopped by to make sure he wasn't sleeping.

As he opened the door he found Lauren standing there.

"You have to be patient."

"She doesn't even see me as a man, Lauren."

"You're going to have to give my innocent friend some extra time and hints."

That's all she said before she walked away.

Innocent, what the fuck did she—his cock went instantly hard as a wave of possessiveness heated his body. No one had ever had —he felt a smile pull at the corners of his mouth. *All mine*, he closed the door and started making plans. The woman would see him as a man no matter what the hell he had to do.

HOW THE FUCK DID SHE ACQUIRE A
NEW FRIEND?

*V*iolet clenched and relaxed her hands as she tried to get through the wedding reception without losing her shit completely. The ceremony turned out perfect, now she had a drunken best man who was determined to give the speech from hell. Bridezilla was fuming, and her new husband was doing everything in his power to keep her calm.

The man was drunk, it would be easy enough to arrange an accident. She felt the evil smile pull at her mouth and she strolled across the room, her target in sight. She slowly passed him as he stumbled about and she bent her right leg at the knee and tripped him. He went down with a groan.

"Oh, are you okay, sir," she sounded concerned. She didn't learn the art of the con in her teens for nothing.

Blood was flowing from his nose. He had landed face first on the floor.

"I'll take him out front and check him out, maybe call the paramedics if I think it's broken. Just enjoy the rest of the reception. I have it all handled."

She helped the man up and steered him toward the front of the banquet room. He was bleeding profusely from his nose and she dialed 911 just to be on the safe side. She waited with him in the lobby, his head leaned back on one of the uncomfortable couches. She held a towel to his nose.

"Violet, are you okay?"

She turned to find Gio jogging toward her and was surprised to see him.

"Best man had a little too much to drink and he had an accident. I wanted to make sure his nose wasn't broken. How did you know to come here?"

"Raven and I were having our dinner break when I heard your name over her radio," he motioned to a beautiful olive-skinned woman in a paramedic uniform.

She was tall and thick, curvy without the obvious lumps and bumps. Maybe that was his type. She'd tried to give an in for Lauren to get a date the other night, but Lauren said she just wanted to be friends. Lauren didn't have time for relationships right now.

"You didn't have to ruin your dinner break."

"I didn't. It's almost time for me to get off shift. We had a few call outs and I missed dinner. Raven shared a table with me. You sure you're okay?"

His concern made her stomach feel odd. Except for Lauren no one cared about her and briefly wondered if that should bother her more than it did.

"I'm good," She lowered her voice and turned, her face in line with his stomach. The man was too damn tall. "I just hope no one saw me trip him."

She bit her bottom lip as he busted out laughing.

"His speech was horrendous, I heard him practicing it. The bride was with me, she scared even me. She's been a nightmare and I wouldn't put it passed her to make her new husband's best friend disappear. Just a few more hours and this hell is over."

"You want to come over and watch a movie when you get home?"

"No, I don't want to be a bother. This fucking bra is killing me. I just want to go home and get in a bath."

"A movie night doesn't require a bra. If you change your mind, just come over and knock."

"I'll see. It'll be late before I get home."

"I have graveyard shifts the next few days. You can keep me awake."

"Okay, do I need to bring anything?"

"Just yourself. I'll pick up chocolate milk on my way home."

She didn't know what to say, so she turned away from him. He pushed in behind her and her body started to do weird things. Thank fuck for industrial strength bras.

"Ma'am, his nose isn't broken, but he really should have someone drive him home." The woman, Raven, spoke as she removed her gloves.

"I'll talk to one of my assistants and make sure he gets home, if they can't do it I—"

"No, you won't, I'll take him home. I'll just call in to sign off duty. See you in a little bit, Violet."

She nodded and felt she should argue about him taking over but guessed she could say they were tentative friends. How the fuck did she acquire a new friend? She'd had one in her life and Lauren knew her since college. Knew how hateful she was and weird.

What could it hurt? The guy was hot and the eye candy wouldn't hurt. If she couldn't have a man of her own at least she could have one she could look at and hang out with.

Gio easily got the man to his feet and was headed toward the front exit. She watched the paramedic follow close behind and before she could think on all the odd shit in her head too much she returned to the reception. Two more hours, she just had to make it a bit longer.

Two hours turned into four and she dragged her feet into her house, quickly showered and changed into comfortable clothes.

Ignored a bra, it wasn't like the man was going to attack her in a fit of lust. It was two friends watching a movie. She slipped her feet into her ducky slippers that quacked as she walked. She made her way next door and knocked. Then she had a thought that maybe he'd gone to bed. The click of the lock told her Gio hadn't already fallen asleep.

He opened the door with a smile, "I was wondering when you'd get home."

Was she supposed to talk because all she could focus on was furry eight pack abs and pajama bottoms that were dangerously close to coming off trim hips.

He chuckled and she jerked her gaze up to his face. He lifted his big hand and wrapped it around her nape to tug her inside.

"I just put popcorn on the table and poured you a big glass of milk. You like horror movies?"

"Is it gory?"

"Yes and I think all the perky chicks die at the beginning."

"Now you're just talking dirty."

Violet loved the sound of his laugh. It was deep and rich, with just the right amount of rumble in the man's barrel chest. She never remembered analyzing a man's laugh before.

"I'm curious about something?"

"What's that?"

"Why the chocolate milk? You do seem a bit obsessed with it."

"Growing up we had to earn things. Not too many treats, so, when I went to college I tried everything I wanted to and some were okay, but chocolate milk was the best. Chocolate flavored drinks paled in comparison."

It wasn't the complete story, but she didn't want to tell him that she'd never been good enough to earn the things her brothers had. She'd stolen things in her teens, candy bars, beer, snacks. More often than not, her brothers beat her to take them. When she'd gone away to college no one could take anything away from her. A bottle of chocolate milk and a pack of stale donuts were the first thing she'd bought herself, it had been heaven. There had been born her addiction to the creamy choco-latey goodness.

She walked into the living room and her slippers quacked, she suddenly felt a little self-conscious about her lack of bra and her choice of slippers. Maybe she should've worn—no, Gio didn't see her like that. No one could, she was too broken.

"Get comfortable."

When he released the back of her neck his hand stroked down her back and stopped at the big swells of her ass. She rushed around the sofa and took a seat on one end, while he took the other side.

"Relax, this is for you to decompress after a shit evening. Come here," he said as he stretched his arm out along the back of the couch and patted his side with his opposite hand.

She inched closer and her arm met his warm skin and the coarse tight curls on his chest and stomach, teased her. What the fuck was she doing?

"Better," he said as he pushed play and the movie started.

Was she supposed to focus? Because that shit wasn't going to happen. All the men she'd been close to were soft and average, they didn't have deeply tanned skin or muscle on top of muscle.

She fisted her hand as she thought about stroking over those hair-roughened muscles to see if they were real. Her gaze skimmed lower from his stomach to the front of his pajama bottoms the outline of the man's package was clear, that was gag toy size. Real men didn't have—she brought her attention to the movie and tried to pretend she wasn't just checking out what he was rocking in his pants.

That would never fit, now she was thinking about the fit. She mentally screamed and with the first killing she was drawn into the movie. Nothing like a horror movie to clear her head.

DID THE WOMAN EVEN KNOW?

*G*io's dick was on high alert and his balls were aching like a fucker. He was rethinking his bright idea of having Violet curl up against his side as they watched the movie. The invite earlier an act of desperation just to get some alone time with Violet. Let her get used to him and learn about him, same as he would with her. He hadn't expected what her heavy breasts would feel like against his side. They were soft and one of her hard nipples pushed against his skin.

A few more minutes and his cock was going to peek up from the waistband of his loose sleep pants. He was a commando kind of guy so even if he had thought about underwear the most he had were boxers he occasionally slept in. Those wouldn't be any type of protection or cover for his hard on.

She was acting like it was nothing. For all she cared she could be curled up to one of her girlfriends watching the movie. He claimed not to be vain but he discovered he really was. He'd almost thought she was interested because when he'd answered the door she'd stared at his stomach with a bit of awe or what he thought was awe. She was short so when he opened the door the first thing she'd see were his upper abs which were at her eye level and he had taken off his shirt to tease her—to see if her hazel eyes turned dark with lust. Again nothing.

He sighed as he raised his hand and rested his cheek on his palm. Women liked him. When he flirted they returned the interest, what about him was so unattractive to Violet that she looked at him like a girlfriend with fucking chest hair?

Maybe he should've made himself clearer that he wanted movie night to be somewhat of a first date.

"You okay, you tensed up, am I too heavy?"

"No, you're perfect, keep watching the movie I need to use the bathroom."

She instantly sat up and moved out of his way, allowing to him push to his feet. He made his way to the downstairs bathroom. He closed the door and rested his hands on the cool sink. He studied himself in the mirror, turning his head left to right. Because of his job and needing his mask to have a seal he never let his facial hair get to be more than a little scruff. He knew some of the guys wore beards, even some of his brothers did, but he'd always avoided a beard. Better safe than sorry.

His body was powerfully built, he worked hard to keep in shape because again his job required it. Everything he had done was for his job, but he was tired of coming home to an empty house. Going to bed alone every night. He was in his late thirties, the second to oldest of his brothers, and he hadn't had a girlfriend last more than a handful of months. His job was important and it took a lot of his time, he took pride in it.

He just didn't understand Violet, didn't she even know he liked her?

He washed his hands and splashed water on his face, then exited the bathroom. He returned to the living room and froze behind the couch. Violet was curled up in a ball fast asleep. He smiled as he softly walked around the sofa, and gently moved her until he could sit back down. He rested her head on his thigh and then pulled the blanket from the back of the couch to place it over her. He combed his fingers through her soft hair, it was thick and heavy in his hand.

She looked so cute in sleep. Her usual irritation nowhere to be seen, plus that adorable little twitch under her eye—shit, he had it bad if he thought her eye twitch was adorable. Against his better judgment he liked her, weird quirks, rage and all.

He knew part of her story from when he'd eavesdropped on her and Lauren. It wasn't a home life that fostered a sense of self-worth. He had a feeling that growing up with a father and brothers who used violence as a means of establishing hierarchy that she didn't see herself as a woman. Even with her pretty dresses and cute shoes, she was just one of the guys.

He thought back to the way she looked when he'd walked into the lobby of the hotel. She'd worn a beautiful, long sheath of silk that flowed over her curves and sexy little stiletto heels. Her cleavage on display for all to see and he had hated that anyone else saw her like that.

Never one to be possessive of a woman, it had taken him by surprise and he'd wanted her to spend the evening with him. He loved her in that sexy dress from earlier, but to be honest, her in a baggy t-shirt and sleep pants, with yellow ducky slippers was just as much of a turn on. The fact that she wasn't wearing a bra and her breasts bounced with every breath or step she took made it better. He was a big man and he knew her curves would over-flow his hands, but she was tiny too. He felt protective of her.

He jerked his phone off the end table before it rang a second time and answered.

"Hey, Ma," he whispered.

"Oh, am I disturbing you?"

"No, my neighbor came over to watch a movie and she fell asleep, I didn't want to wake her. What's up?"

"A woman neighbor, what to tell me something, son?"

He quietly chuckled at his mother's amused tone. One thing him and his brothers learned growing up was that their parents would always be there. As long as they were doing what made them happy then they'd always be proud of them.

"No, I don't. Especially not right now."

"Deal, I'll wait until she isn't around to drag all the information out of you. Is this the woman Renz said brought you donuts at the house and you were rude?"

"I wasn't rude to her, Ma. Renz shouldn't be telling stories."

As he spoke he kept stroking his fingers along her arm, then down to her hip and retraced the path. The motions soothed his chaotic thoughts.

"I'm just going to say, me and your father didn't raise you to be rude to ladies."

"I know, so, what are you doing calling me after midnight?"

"You have graveyard shifts coming up, so I wanted to make sure you were staying awake."

"I am, that's why I invited Violet over to keep me company. She's an event coordinator. Shit, I should've asked if she had to work tomorrow."

"Let her sleep a bit longer and then you can wake her and send her home. Unless you carry her upstairs and tuck her in with you for the night."

"Is it weird that my mother is trying to get me to take my female friend upstairs to bed?"

"No, because I know my boys and we never made you and your brothers ashamed of sex."

"Hold on," He took a quick picture of Violet and sent it to his mother. "There, to appease your nosiness."

He chuckled softly at his mother's girly squeal and shook his head.

"She's so cute, son, you must bring her to visit so I can meet her."

"I'll think about it."

"Don't be mean to me, I'll tell your father."

"I'm almost forty and you're still pulling the I'm going to tell your father card."

"Yeah, it's always worked. Okay, your dad is glaring at me. He keeps reminding me he's retired and I don't have to stay up all night anymore."

"Get some sleep, Ma, tell dad hi and I love you both."

"We love you too, son."

He disconnected the call and set his phone aside, he looked down at Violet to find her watching him. The back of her head rested on his thigh.

"Hey, shit, I didn't mean to wake you."

He hadn't wanted to wake her because he knew as soon as she did she'd want to go home. He was enjoying her company even with her asleep. He loved having her presence in his house. He imagined this was what it would be like to have a girlfriend.

"You didn't."

"You okay?"

"Yeah, I better get home."

She started to get up and he laid his arm across her to keep her in place. His forearm snug between her breasts. The blanket molding to them and he almost shifted his arm to curve his hand around the plump side. He wanted to test the weight in his palm and strum his thumb across the clearly hard nipple.

"You have to work?"

"No, weekends are my own when I don't have to attend events. I don't have another one until next Saturday."

"Then just lay there and watch the movie, I'll wake you when I head to bed."

"Your parents still tell you they love you?"

She had a blank look on her face.

"Yeah, every time I see them or we talk."

"I thought that was just on TV."

"Your parents didn't—"

"My mom thought I was too short and frail, so my dad and

brothers took it upon themselves to toughen me up. By the time I was ten I could take a punch with a smile."

It broke a piece of him at how easily she spoke of being abused by her parents and siblings. The part of him that wanted to care for her—make her his—urged him to try and erase the bad. He couldn't do that, though. The past he had begun to hate was what made Violet her and despite first impressions he liked the odd woman.

"Baby, that's not how families are supposed to work."

"I know that. I told some friends at school, I think I was eleven or so, they asked about a black eye. I told them with pride that my brother looked worse. They looked at me like I was weird."

"There's nothing wrong with you, baby, just because you're short doesn't mean you're frail."

"The top of my head only reaches the top of your stomach."

"Nothing wrong with that, not everyone can be freakishly tall like me."

He felt lighter when she smiled, but he didn't like the way she turned away to hide it.

"Where are your parents?"

"Mom is a pit boss in Vegas. I haven't talked to her in a few years. Dad is in court ordered rehab. My brothers are in jail, three of them are in for a drug deal that went bad and the other is in for beating his wife. I sold most of my stuff to move her across the country and get her settled before he comes up for parole."

"Why did you have to sell all your stuff?"

Violet had a deep layer of sweetness that not everyone was privileged to witness.

"I went to dad for the money, I had a stash for emergencies. He found out about it, cleaned it out, so I went to get it back. It didn't go down quite like I thought it would."

"What happened?"

"You never forget the day you come face to face with the barrel of a shotgun."

"Violet."

"Don't fucking pity me. I can take care of myself."

"Yeah, you took me down and not many people can do that."

"I probably took you by surprise. A five-foot size twenty woman coming at you. I wish I could remember the look on your face."

Her laugh was loud and made her breasts sway, her cheeks turned pink with amusement.

"You blackout often?"

Her brow furrowed as she seemed to think about how to answer. "No, first time I remember doing it, but it could've happened before, I get mad a lot."

"Have you been mad tonight?"

This time he knew she was thinking. He registered her confusion and he knew her answer before she even parted the curves of her mauve-colored lips.

"No," she appeared shocked by her own answer. "I'm always mad. You learn to hide it well, but I haven't been angry once. It's—"

"It's what?"

"Weird."

"Good weird?"

"Yeah, good."

"Why don't you come to dinner at my parents place? They do it every Sunday, we show up when we're not working. Right now, I plan to go next week. Want to come?"

"Really, meet your family, do you think that's wise?"

"My family will love you. Say yes and then I won't have to bug you all week."

"I guess I can do that."

"Neither of us paid much attention to the movie, I'm going to restart it. If you fall asleep again I'll just cover you up and leave you on the couch."

"Okay."

She was quiet after that and he restarted the movie from the beginning. He was too aware of her, every breath she took. The movements of her body next to him. He even lifted her hair as he stroked it just to feel the softness of it against his stomach. He didn't hide it when his body reacted, but he also didn't point it out. When she stretched her right arm over her head to lay across his knees, he took her hand in his and laced their fingers. It was torture but he wouldn't change it. He wanted the little woman in his bed, but he'd be patient and give her all the time she needed. Maybe he'd finally found his one.

HOLY SHIT, DIDN'T HE OWN CLOTHES?

Over the last two weeks if she wasn't at work she found herself at Gio's place. She'd had to miss the family dinner he'd invited her to, but that was because she'd taken over a Sunday Charity Event from a sick co-worker. She changed into her comfortable clothes and walked outside after hearing Gio talking with someone in the backyard.

Land of Giants, she froze as she saw Gio bent over with a lineup of him and three men on one side and four on the opposite side facing off. She jumped out of the way as they scrambled and a football sailed through the air. A man passed too close to her and knocked into her, she clenched her fists and growled.

"Violet!"

She calmed as soon as she heard Gio's voice. She glanced at him to find Gio smiling at her. His eyes shimmered with amusement.

"Unclench the fists."

"I wasn't doing anything."

"Yeah, right."

Gio jogged over to her, he was shirtless and sweaty. Didn't the fucker know what clothes were? Her hormones were in overdrive and she was going through batteries like crazy. The first time she'd spent the night at his house to watch a movie she'd been aware of everything about the man. The way he didn't wear cologne, just smelled like clean soap and deodorant. His rock hard thigh under her head. She swore a few times she'd felt the jump of his cock against the crown of her head.

He threw his arms around her and the thick hair on his stomach cushioned her cheek.

"Come, let me introduce you to my brothers and a friend."

He didn't release her just turned her, his arms draped down her body, his forearms pushing to her hard nipples. She was going to have to start wearing her industrial strength bras in his company.

"Violet, you met Renz, but that's Sal, Nicco, Montes, and Maximo, Tony, and Renz's best friend, Lyn."

Everyone had waved and said hello as they were introduced, all the brothers looked alike and were built on the same scale except Montes, he was even bigger and wider than his already massive brothers. Lyn was slender and soft looking.

"Hi."

"We were wondering who was keeping our brother away." Sal said with a friendly smile.

"I didn't do anything." She didn't understand why she suddenly felt defensive as if she'd done something wrong by spending time with Gio. It was Gio's decision to invite her over.

"Don't let them give you shit, as someone who's been around the Masiello brothers for twenty years too long they live to be assholes."

She smiled at Lyn as the man winked at her.

"Lyn, hands off."

She tipped her head back to find Gio glaring at Lyn.

"Dude, have we forgotten I'm gay?"

"I forget that because when's the last time you had a boyfriend?"

Lyn groaned and Renz instantly wrapped his arm around the other man's waist. Lyn leaned into Renz and she wondered if there was something going on there.

"I don't want to talk about it."

"Exactly," Gio said with a chuckle.

She listened with amusement as they kept giving each other shit. None of her brothers ever bantered like this without it turning into a brawl that most of the time required stitches or x-rays.

"Stay for guy's night, we just finished our game, next was food and Renz chose video games for tonight's entertainment," Gio offered.

"Gio, it's guys night, I can just head home."

She'd gotten used to spending her evenings with him when he wasn't working. It was nice to pass time with someone other than Lauren. She loved her best friend but the woman really was all sunshine and positive thoughts. It annoyed her and Lauren understood it. It was one of the reasons they'd been friends as long as they had. Lauren knew her limits and what she could take.

"No, come on, at least keep me company. I suck at video games."

"That's because you're old and your reflexes are shit," Renz smirked.

"I got fifty he can kick your ass." She was surprised by the challenge before it had fully slipped passed her lips.

"Oh, we're going to get serious tonight. You're on, woman."

She growled and Gio's fingers sunk into her soft stomach as she started to go after Renz. She hated when people called her woman or pet names, Gio called her baby but that was different, it was Gio.

"Keep the woman comments to a minimum please. She tackled my ass when I made the mistake."

"Is that what you said?"

"That and I ordered you to turn down your fucking music."

"It's good music."

"It's screaming."

"Just because you have no taste."

"Come on, I have to win my girl fifty bucks." Gio turned his back to her, "Hop on." She rolled her eyes, twined her arms around his neck and he carried her into the house piggyback style.

"No, no, you don't get a lucky charm to sit on your lap."

She listened to Renz complain behind her and the other brothers giving Renz shit. Gio kept one hand on her ass as he opened the door and walked into the kitchen, then let the door bang closed behind them. Leaving the others to open it and enter. She was placed on the counter beside the sink as he dug into his junk drawer for all the takeout menus.

"She won't be on my lap, she'll be sitting on the floor between my legs. That's different. You got your best friend, let me have mine."

It was a compliment and a slap all in one, she'd been put into the friend category. Not that she hadn't expected it, but, damn, couldn't he have left her with her delusions.

"You're in charge of picking dinner, baby, what do you want?"

He moved to stand between her knees, handed her the stack of menus, and rested his hands on the counter beside her hips. She went through them and went with the safe option of Chinese even though the Thai food appealed to her more. She never really had to worry about other people except Lauren before. It was odd to consider what others might like.

"Is that what you want?"

"Yeah."

"Are you sure?"

"Just order the damn food."

He wrote down her order and his, then threw the notepad toward the table as the other guys read the menu and chose.

"You're a bossy little thing."

"I'm not bossy." She rolled her eyes as he arched a heavy brow and she jerked as his fingers played along her ribs.

"Is someone ticklish?"

"I will kill you in your sleep."

"That means you'd be in my room, I might risk it."

He hugged her to his chest and his lips pressed to her temple, she couldn't resist when she leaned into the caress of his lips.

"Baby," He whispered in her ear.

"Yeah," she played with the curls on his belly without looking at him.

"You keep touching me like that and I'm sending my brothers and friend home."

She pulled back putting distance between them, she looked up at him from under her lashes and stroked her fingers lower to the elastic waistband of his shorts.

"I dare you," he said with a smirk.

Oh, dares were serious business, and she'd never turned one down in her life no matter how dangerous it was. She darted her gaze to the other people in the room and found them not paying attention to her and Gio. She stroked her tongue along her bottom lip and she was surprised by her boldness. She slipped her fingers beneath the elastic, felt the tighter curls at the base of his cock and his huge hands tightened painfully on her hips. Her teeth sunk into her lower lip as she grazed her fingertips along hot silky skin.

His rough cheek teased hers.

"You're playing with fire, a few more minutes and you're going to get yourself fucked. If you're not ready to find yourself on my dick you might want to stop."

She drew back, her lips teasing the corner of his mouth and she retreated as he tried to kiss her.

His hand wrapped around the back of her neck, his fingertips digging into her skin, and his forehead pressed to hers. His breathing was ragged, his dick tented the front of his shorts, and his mouth came closer to hers. Drawing out the anticipation.

"Is that what you want, baby? Me to pound that sweet little body into my mattress? You know these walls are thin. You scream when you cum, little girl."

"You—you've been listening?"

"You've gotten louder since you met me." His words were a tease against her lips, "You're going to be a good girl until they leave and then I'll let you take care of what you did."

Gio moved his body closer and he groaned when his dick pressed into her stomach. She didn't know what she was supposed to do, yeah, she flicked the bean a lot, but she was single and horny. She'd never thought of finding someone who actually wanted her. Nervousness and excitement tightened her stomach, her panties were soaked.

She was tugged off the counter and set gently on her feet. His cock pushed into her upper stomach. He pressed a lingering kiss to her mouth before he turned and left the room.

"Best friend my ass," One of the brothers muttered and they all wandered out of the room.

She collapsed back against the counter and lifted her hand to her mouth. Traced the curves of her lips. Shit, she glanced towards the back door and wondered if she could escape.

"Don't you dare run, baby," Gio yelled from somewhere in the house and she heard the challenge, the dare in his tone.

She didn't run, he could do his worst.

HIS LITTLE GIRL WANTED TO PLAY

*V*iolet was right where he said she'd be, sitting between his legs on the floor and with his arms around her. He didn't resist touching her. His big hand cupped her breast, the touch was blocked by his legs and arms. She trembled as he played with her hard nipple. He rolled it between his thumb and forefinger. He smiled at her gasp before she caught herself. His company was too engrossed in the game to pay attention to them.

He ached and he could swear there was a wet spot on his shorts, but he didn't give a fuck. He'd waited too long. Tonight she was his. He leaned farther forward and nipped at the shell of her ear.

"Really, y'all can't wait to continue the foreplay until we leave," Montes growled. "I'm going home, us single men can only deal with so much."

Violet tensed in his arms but he didn't pay his brother any attention. Just continued to touch his woman the way he wanted. He watched her eyes close as he kissed down to her throat. Sucked lightly at her pulse point. He smirked as everyone gathered up their stuff, Renz broke down his game console, and finally they were all gone.

"I ruined guy's night."

He'd thank them later for leaving and buy them all the beer they wanted.

He didn't wait any longer than it took for the lock of the front door to click, he had her straddling his lap. His mouth came down on hers and he reached under her shirt, cupped her bare breasts. They were heavy and laid against her body. He loved she never wore a bra around him.

"Fuck, you're so soft and sexy." He tugged her closer until his cock notched between her pussy lips through her thin pants. He could feel the heat and wetness. "Shit, baby, you're soaked."

He ripped her shirt over her head and he groaned as she whimpered when her breasts flattened to his chest. He rubbed his hairy skin against her and her nipples pulled even tighter. He kissed her as she rocked against his dick. Her arms wrapped around his neck, she hugged his head and roughly sank her fingers into his hair. The burn at his scalp made his hips jerk upward. His tongue pushed deeper into her mouth. He traced the sharp edges of her teeth. Violet's ragged breathing rushed hot against his cheek.

He flipped them until she was under him on the couch, she was so tiny she was rubbing her pussy against his stomach.

"I want in you, now."

He reached between them and hooked his hand in the waistband of her pants, tearing them roughly down her legs. It was awkward stripping away the last of her clothes, but he could bear to let her go.

Fuck, he hadn't seen anything that sexy in his fucking life. Her pubic curls were thick, a perfect triangle of dark hair. With her legs open wide he could see the glistening lightly furred lips. Shit he hadn't seen a natural pussy in forever. He covered her fully with his hand and pushed his fingers between her slick labia, he breached her with one finger. Her hips jackknifed off the cushion and she cried out.

"That's right, baby girl, ride my finger." He used his thumb to tease the hard nub of her clit.

Fingering her he shifted until he stood and pushed his shorts off.

"Oh, no, my toys aren't that big."

He heard a slight twinge of fear in her voice and she started to move away, but he curled his finger inside her, locking in place.

"Baby, you'll be good and ready before I take you. I wouldn't hurt you for the world. Our first time isn't going to be rough and quick, that's for later after I've got you nice and used to taking my cock."

There was a rush of fluid around his finger and it pooled in his palm.

"That's right, little girl, give it all to me."

He knelt on the floor, placed her leg over his shoulder as he replaced his thumb with his tongue. Her flavor filled his mouth, sweet and musky. He could eat her all night and be a happy man. Her soft dimpled thighs squeezed his head as she squealed and whimpered as she rode his mouth and finger. His free hand went to her breasts, curled his hand over the top of the left one and clasped the heavy softness.

She was everything he'd ever wanted in a lover and didn't know it. She was soft and full, her curves gave and allowed him to mold them. Her body moved and jiggled as she writhed. He pushed a second finger in to join the other, gently stretching her. She was fucking tight and as much as he wanted to feel her wrapped snug around his cock. He wouldn't hurt her. She should never have anything but pleasure from him. He sucked on and off her clit as she clawed at his scalp.

He couldn't take anymore. He pulled his fingers from her pussy, licked them as she watched him under heavy eyelids. He picked her up and she wrapped her legs around him, locking her ankles. There was no way he could resist kissing her as he made his way to his bedroom. He stopped at the top of the stairs and pressed her back to the wall, the tip of his cock pushed between her lips. Against his will he thrust, feeling the resistance of her pussy.

He groaned as he reached under her thigh and grabbed the base of his cock, he held it as he thrust. He broke the kiss as she screamed and his head rolled back as her pussy strangled the first few inches of his dick.

He shallowly fucked her, torturing himself with the feel of his bare cock surrounded by her.

He studied her face, her eyes were squeezed closed and her lips were parted. Her hips were arched forward and she was so tense her muscles shook, her heels dug into his lower back.

"S'tight," he hissed between clenched teeth, "S'fucking good, baby girl. Made for my dick," he groaned as he slammed his hips upward until he was balls deep. "Oh shit, baby, are—" His question was cut off as she rolled her hips and ground down on his cock. His dick jerked and the pleasure bordered on pain. Shit, he had to get to his bedroom.

He didn't pull out, he enjoyed a moment of feeling her bare and wet, hot and silky around him.

"We need a condom now." His voice harsh with the strain as she bounced on his cock as he rushed for his room. He finally pushed through his bedroom door, laid her gently on the bed and reluctantly eased out of her.

He stood beside his bed as he stared down at her. Her hand cupped her breasts, played with her nipples and he could see she was all slick and wet, her inner thighs shimmered with her cream. He looked down at his cock and saw the evidence of her need slicked along his shaft, glistening in the curls at his thick base. His hands shook as jerked open his drawer and found a condom, checked the date. It had been too long since he'd needed one.

He tore open the packet, pinched the tip and rolled it down his length. He turned back to the bed just in time to catch her playing with her little clit. Stroking her fingertips just over the tip of her clit.

"No, that's all mine, baby."

"It was mine first."

He fell onto the bed and licked over her hard nub that peeked from between her caressing fingers.

"Now, it's all mine."

"I need bigger toys, you're going to ruin me."

"No more toys, unless I get to watch you play with them," he smirked as he crawled up her body. "Have you done this before, baby?" He knew Lauren said she was innocent, but with how sexy she was he had his doubts. She dropped her gaze from his. "No, don't be shy, I had you on my cock a few minutes ago. I should've been gentler."

"No one's ever wanted me and I won't break."

"Is that a challenge?"

"It is what it is."

He growled as he wrapped his hand around his cock and lined up, "You're mine from the day forward, you understand what that means?"

"I got a boyfriend now."

He wanted to wipe that teasing smile off her sexy mouth.

"Fucking right," he slammed all the way in and loved the way her body arched, she let out a long, low moan. He rode her hard as she wrapped her hands under his headboard. Her breasts swayed as he thrust deeper and firmer. His hips had her thighs pushed all the way to the sides, almost flat to the mattress. Fuck, she was so small compared to him.

He held himself up to watch his cock disappearing into her red, stretched hole.

"Fuck, you're sexy, all split wide."

He pulled out and flipped her to her hands and knees.

"Not like this—"

He brought his hand down on her pale ass cheek and it wobbled just right. "I want to see this ass bounce as I fuck it." He thrust back into her as he grabbed her hips, every slam of his cock into her and he watched the sexy jiggle of her ass. Then she was cursing and slamming back onto his cock, he held still and let her fuck herself onto him.

"Spank me again, fucking do it," she demanded.

"Anything my girl wants." He spanked one cheek then the other, over and over, felt the way her pussy clenched around him with each strike.

"My toys never felt like this."

Even as he smiled his balls ached and he was so close, he reached around her and spanked her pretty swollen lips. She fell forward and she whimpered, begged him to make her cum. He pinched her abused clit and her scream was music to his fucking ears. She tightened so fucking rigid around him that he groaned in pain, he wrapped his hands around her hips and rode her hard, thrust his cock into her pussy repeatedly until he couldn't hold back. He slammed his hips to her ass one more time and spilled into the condom. He blanketed her back, curled his arms under her and curved his hands over her shoulders. He fucked into her in shallow thrusts until it was too much and he stilled, savored the rhythmic pulses of her body around his still half hard cock.

"Shit, baby," He kissed her sweaty cheek and felt her thighs tremble against his and then he noticed she was moving her hips, whimpering. "You want to cum again?"

She nodded her head and her cheek rubbed against his, he smoothed his hand down the center of her body, over the rounded plane of her stomach. He gently rubbed her clit knowing she was too sensitive after the pussy spanking and she jerked.

"Such a good girl, getting off so hard for me, but you want more, and I'll always give you what you want."

He started slow and tender, building the pressure until she was bucking under him. He loved the way she ground down on his cock.

"I—"

She cut herself off and he watched her teeth sink into her bottom lip.

"What is it, all you have to do is ask and it's yours."

"Would you—"

"Would I what?"

"Play with my ass."

His spent cock jerked and he didn't waste time, he straightened, still stroking her clit. He gathered up some of her wetness on the fingertips of his free hand, brought it back to her tight hole, the wrinkled skin resisted the prod of his thick finger. When it gave her back arched up and she flooded around his cock still buried inside her.

"Oh, baby girl, you were fucking made for me," He eased his finger and cock from her, eased her down onto the bed.

Her hair was stuck to her sweaty face and she was splayed across his bed. He left her only long enough to dispose of the condom, clean up and get a warm wet rag to clean her up. As he washed her swollen pussy he studied her. He set the cloth on the floor beside the bed and he laid down beside her, drew her into his arms. She threw her thigh over his.

"You okay, baby?"

She hummed and her plump lips pulled into a satisfied smile, a man couldn't get a better compliment than that.

"And I didn't think you liked me."

"I thought the same. I've wanted you since you showed me that sexy ass that first night."

"Oh fuck, I still can't believe I did that."

"Thank you for letting me be your first."

"My toys were the first."

He loved the argument because it was so Violet.

"Break my heart why don't you?"

"Sorry," she laughed.

"Let's get some sleep, I don't work tomorrow, so I expect morning sex."

"As you wish."

He kissed her forehead, her nose and then her mouth. He smiled as she cuddled against his side as she got comfortable. Her breathing quickly evened out and he laid there savoring her warmth and the weight of her. She doesn't know it yet, but he was going to keep her. He hadn't lied when he said she was made for him. It was quick, but he didn't care. Only a month had passed since his woman had tackled him but he noticed the difference between the way she reacted to him and others. She didn't feel angry with him. She was open and let him shower her with affection.

Violet had to feel something for him. He'd give her time to get used to being his, but in his gut he knew she was it for him. He pulled the covers over them and he closed his eyes, pressed one more kiss to her forehead before he let himself relax enough to sleep.

VIOLET NEVER DID A MORNING AFTER BEFORE

A big body was curled up around her when Violet woke up. Strong arms held her tight and just as she was about to scoot to the edge of the bed and escape the night before flashed in her head. Shit, she'd slept with Gio, hot, gorgeous firefighter, what the fuck had she been thinking? He's seen her in all her unshaved and natural glory. The fucking man lived beside her. She saw him almost every day. They were friends for fuck's sake. Oh fuck, he saw her naked.

"If you're going to run, make coffee before you leave," Gio's voice husky as he scooted up closer behind her. "Or option two, we have morning sex, and then you make coffee before you run."

"No wonder you're single, your sweet morning talk has me so swoony and weak in the knees."

The rough chuckle that ruffled her hair caused her to smile. "Good thing you're laying down then. So, what about that morning sex?" His big rough hand squeezed her breast like he was honking a fucking horn.

She growled and rolled, pushing him to his back so she could straddle his hips.

"Got that running shit out of your head," he smugly smiled up at her and crossed his arms under his head.

"Why do I like you again?" She crossed her arms under her breasts and watched his gaze lock on the plumped oversized curves.

"Because I'm sexy?"

His fingertips teased her nipples causing them to tighten into big hard nubs. If she had anything she was self-conscious about, it was her nipples. Those bastards when erect could be seen from outer space.

"Nope, seen sexier."

"Because you like my dick?"

To emphasize his point he pushed the base of his cock deeper between her plump pussy lips.

"It's alright, a little crooked and really dicks ain't pretty. Besides I can get better at the sex shop."

"You a Pro-Domme or something, because, damn, you could get paid a fortune for your humiliation techniques alone."

"I have been thinking of a career change."

Why the fuck was she so happy just sitting there on his morning hard on and talking? She hated everyone except Lauren, but that woman was her best friend. She hadn't known Gio long enough for the level of absent irritation. Even the honking of her breast and his smug look only amused her. She uncrossed her arms and drew patterns on his hairy stomach with her nails.

"Why were you thinking of running?"

She huffed and threw her head back, stared up at the ceiling wondering if she wanted to tell him the truth or a version of it. Gio's hands cupped her hips and moved up to her sides, they were so big they covered her ribs. Gio gave her a little shake.

"Talk."

She lifted her head and brought her chin to her chest. "I've seen all those women who shave, wax and pluck every stray fucking hair. I wiggle."

"I like when you wiggle," He used his thumbs to push against the underside of her breasts and cause them to bounce.

"You're weird."

"Not weird, unique, and why the fuck do women have to live up to every bizarre fad that's reported as the new sexy thing? So, you're not shaved bare, if people like it that's their thing. That doesn't mean everyone has got to do it. I happen to love every curve and hair. Or didn't I prove that enough last night?"

She looked down to watch one fingertip stroke the line of fine, pale hair that went from her bellybutton over the curve of her lower stomach to the top of her bush. She watched his expression. Studying the changes, the way he licked his lips and the tight curve of his mouth. His cock jerked beneath her and she couldn't help when her hips rolled.

"If that's what I wanted, I'd find it, but it's not and I won't regret that last night I had my head between your thighs licking those fuzzy pussy lips or my cock buried inside you. I've wanted you since you tackled me. I won't be ashamed that I like the woman sitting here straddling my hips talking to me."

"Shouldn't the morning after be all flowery and romantic, or awkwardness paired with a walk of shame?"

She'd always assumed her first time would be her walking out of some strange guy's or a boyfriend's place to never call or be called again. She hadn't expected to be sitting there naked and talking like it was any other day. She reluctantly admitted to herself she liked it. She really liked Gio.

"I don't want you ashamed when you walk out my door. If you are then I didn't make you feel like I should've. Don't get me wrong, I hadn't planned last night and I thought I was just a girl-friend with chest hair. I was pleasantly surprised to find out I didn't have to pretend that I didn't want you or what happened."

She flinched slightly as he stretched out his arm and reached into the open drawer of the nightstand. He removed a condom and he nudged her stomach with his free hand. She observed his every move as he ripped open the packet, slid the condom on and tapped her hip.

"Hop on, we're going to play a game."

"That sounds like the start to a bad horror movie." He snorted and seemed to ignore her sarcasm.

"First one to break has to make coffee and breakfast."

She rolled her eyes as she wrapped her fingers around the base, holding him up and she moaned a little at the slight discomfort as she lowered herself down the thick length.

"If you're sore we—"

"Hey, just because my toys aren't made with Giant cock molds doesn't mean I can't handle it."

"Yes, ma'am."

Gio's ma'am broke off in a deep groaned as he pushed his head back into the pillows.

Oh, she liked that, she closed her eyes at the stretch and the small twinge of pain. She was a lot smaller than Gio and for the first time in her life she was happy for her lack of height. She loved how delicate Gio made her feel it was a new and novel experience. His thick bush teased her clit as she settled her weight fully on him.

She started to move her hips and he grabbed them in a bruising grip.

"Don't move, just be still."

How the fuck was she supposed to stay still?

"What's your favorite color?" His tone was strained and almost sounded like he was in pain.

"Don't make fun of me, I like pink."

"Why would I make fun," he groaned and his entire body shuddered, seeming to work upward from his toes, "Fuck, I wouldn't make fun of you."

She felt a slow smile spread across her mouth as she noticed him breaking out in a sweat. She tightened around him a few times, sucking in her stomach not to hide it but to grip his dick as hard as she could. She shivered at the pleasure, but he was worse off. He threw his arms over his head and wrapped his big hands under the headboard.

"I said no moving."

"I didn't move."

"What do you fucking call that pussy clench you just did? That's called cheating."

"No that's called an involuntary reflex to having a huge object inside me."

"Now, I'm huge?"

She ignored his question, "What's your favorite color?"

He removed one of his hands from the headboard and cupped one of her breasts, he stroked over her nipple. "Dusky mauve, the color of your nipples, and both sets of those beautiful lips."

She took a shuddering breath, "Isn't touching me cheating?" A sheen of sweat broke out over her body.

"You clenched that pussy, you changed the rules."

"Is that right," she laid her hands flat on his ridged stomach and canted her hips back and forth. His thickness dragged along the inside of her pleasure clenched pussy. "Interesting, if I can change the rules, why not? I've never been much a rule follower."

His hand curved over the front of her thigh and his fingertips sunk into the softness.

"I can see you're a com—" Gio growled, "Complete rebel. You should have an anarchy tattoo."

"I'll put it on my list."

She squeaked as he sat up and pressed his lips to hers, "You want to play, little girl, let's play."

She didn't have time to respond or think, and he flipped them and started to pound her into the mattress.

She whispered against his lips, "I won."

"Baby, don't get used to it, now, scream my fucking name."

He slammed into her again, forcing a choked scream to tear from her throat and all arrogance over her win fled.

SHE WAS GOING TO GET TIRED OF HIS EXCUSES

*I*t was a month of excuses, they called him in or there was a last minute schedule change. Gio knew she was going to get tired of him sooner or later changing their dates. She hadn't been in his bed since their first night together. How could one night make him miss her sleeping presence beside him?

He was exhausted and he scrubbed his hands over his face.

They'd gone on a few dates, mostly during the day on her lunch breaks and he loved the times they talked. She'd started a habit of calling him when she got ready for bed.

He was just waiting for her to say she wanted someone who could be there with a normal schedule. His brother's wife, Esther, was used to sometimes being second to a demanding job. She'd grown up with emergency service demands, she was related to cops, paramedics and firefighters.

It was keeping in shape, working shifts all over the place and not to mention, being on duty for sometimes days like he was tonight. When Tony wasn't on shift the man showered his wife and son with every ounce of love the man possessed.

Never had he ever regretted his job until he had to tell his woman that he was called in or leave suddenly during dinner when all hands were required. She smiled and just told him to be careful, but every time he couldn't stop himself from searching for disappointment. He never saw it. That didn't mean she wasn't one hell of an actress. Violet did make it through her days without killing anyone and he knew she'd plotted hundreds, maybe thousands of deaths over the years all the while sweetly smiling in her mental victims faces.

He stared down into his coffee as he pushed his plate of half-eaten food aside. He was in his favorite twenty-hour diner, frequented a lot by emergency service personnel. When he'd walked inside, instead of joining a table of his friends he'd found a booth in back. He needed quiet and time to think, but maybe time to think was a bad idea. All he had learned from thinking too much was the certainty that Violet would get bored and leave him.

"Oh shit, Gio Masiello is frowning."

He looked up at the sound of a familiar teasing voice and found a friend of the family's—Alvin—better known by their drag name Hella Ticked. She was in full drag and looked tired. He stood and motioned to the other side of the booth.

"Hella, didn't take some hot Bear home with you tonight?"

"If I did, would I be here for food at 3 a.m.?" She slid onto the bench seat across from him.

"True."

"Is it okay if sit with you?" Hella asked as she looked around.

He waved over the waitress and waited while Hella ordered a milkshake and the biggest burger they offered along with a double order of fries. He swore he didn't know how Hella didn't gain a pound, Hella was the same height and size from when they were in high school together. Maybe even a bit skinnier. He waited for the woman to walk away before he reached across the table to take Hella's hand.

"Hella, no one will ever tell me who I should be friends with. I love you just like my brothers."

"Shame."

He smiled at her wistful sigh and shook his head. He relaxed against the back cushion.

"You'll find the hairy Sasquatch of your dreams one of these days."

"I can dream and I do a lot of it. So, what's got you so down?"

He didn't even question telling his friend what bothered him, "I'm waiting for my girlfriend to get tired of my bullshit."

"Does this have to do with your job?"

"Yeah, I never really had an issue with my job, but every woman I've dated said I never had enough time for them. I love what I do. I fucking take pride in it. I just don't want Violet to—"

"If she cares and knows how much your job means to you then it shouldn't be a problem. Have you asked how she feels about it?"

"It's still new, we've only been dating a little over a month, but started hanging out a few months ago. I don't want to point out the problems already."

"Well, from my great experience at failed romance, sometimes you shouldn't let all the bullshit fester until it reaches the point where nothing can be done about it."

"How did you get so wise?"

"Honey, if you've gone through as many breakups as me, you'd be a professional by now."

He didn't see any sadness in his friend. Hella was one of those upbeat, perky people that you loved even though they were so positive it was sickening.

"Like I said you'll find him."

"I don't think so, it's all good though. I got freedom, jobs I love, and when I'm at the club all the eye candy I want. So, how did you meet the girlfriend, no one has shared this information with me? Even your brother Renz hasn't been gossiping."

"She hasn't met the parents yet. I think my brothers are giving me a little space before they start hinting. Ma and Pop know, I just haven't gotten around to getting her to their house yet."

"Why not? Ma loves when her boys bring home lovely people for them to meet."

"I keep planning to take her to meet them, but it's just one fuck up after another."

"Just take her, it doesn't have to be for Sunday Family dinner. Pick her up and take her over on a lunch break or one night during the week. You skipped how you met, tell me," Hella demanded as she excepted her food and thanked the waitress.

"I told her to turn down her fucking music and she tackled me, then almost got arrested by the cops."

"She tackled you, are you dating a Giantess?"

"No, she's five foot even."

Hella choked as she laughed and cursed, "Oh shit, a fry went up my nose. Don't do that to a girl when she's eating. Love at first sight?"

"Yes."

Hella's face went blank and her dark, exaggerated brows moved closer to the hairline of her blonde, purple streaked wig.

"You're joking right, you know—"

"I didn't realize when I met her, but she's different and fun, a bit psychotic."

"I like her already."

"I don't have to pretend, we can laugh and have fun. I don't have to be all smooth and debonair. Want to see her?"

"Of course, show me this paragon of psychoses."

He leaned to the side and pulled his phone out, he searched until he found the last picture he'd taken of her. Violet had been laughing and relaxed, he loved her sass and the way she didn't take his shit, but his picture proved he could make her happy. That she didn't need to always be angry and irritated, that she could just be. He turned the screen for Hella to see.

"Fuck, Gio, she's adorable."

"Oh god, please don't say that in her presence."

"I'll refrain, but understand I'll be thinking it. You did good there, sweetie."

"I did, didn't I? She has this love of death metal to help her think. She was playing it and screaming along, I got so pissed that I ran out of the house when she was taking her trash to the curb. I called her woman and told her to turn down her fucking music. She took me out before I knew what was happening." He smiled to himself as he put his phone back to sleep and returned it to his pocket.

"Have you told her yet?"

"You did call her a paragon of psychoses. I know she likes me and that I like her, but it's sorta a weird situation. I don't want to say it because I'm sure she'll run hard and fast in the opposite direction."

"You don't know if you don't try."

He rolled his lips between his teeth, took a deep breath and sighed heavily through his mouth.

"I don't know, my job and the limited time I'm able to spend with her."

"Doesn't mean she doesn't feel the same as you. A lot of cops, firefighters and EMTs have great and happy relationships. Y'all give up a lot to serve your communities. Put your lives on the line. That's something to be respected. And for some reason, I know in my gut that she gets it. So, next time you're able to spend time with her, tell her and take her to your parents. Show her you want to keep her around and that when you're not with her you're still thinking and worrying about her."

He nodded and drifted into silence as he let Hella eat. Maybe Hella was right and he just needed to lay it all out. He was already worried that she was going to break up with him. If he did all the shit Hella suggested then possibly it could end before he got too invested and dreamed of a future with Violet. This wasn't some bullshit romance novel. It wasn't all perfect and laid out. He wasn't going to get love handed to him with some big red bow.

He didn't want that. He wanted real. He wanted all those times they were silly like the morning after they'd had sex, they had laughed and joked. It felt right because it wasn't mired down in the expectations of what a relationship should be between them.

He wrapped his hand around his mug of now cold coffee and brought it to his mouth.

"Gio, you'll do the right thing, because that's the kinda man you and your brothers are. But don't forget that as much as you love your job it's not always going to be there and where will that leave you?"

"Thanks, Hella. I'll bring Violet to the club to meet you one night. She's going to love you."

He liked the smile Hella gifted him with. He knew his friend's life wasn't easy, never had been, but Hella always lived in the positive. He wouldn't deny he needed to have that attitude more than he did.

SHE HAD A FUCKING BOYFRIEND

*V*iolet still couldn't get it through her head even after a month that she was dating a hot and sweet firefighter. She kept waiting for him to grow tired of her surly attitude, her penchant for violence, but she didn't feel any of that when she was with him. They talked, went on dates when his schedule allowed, but she kept putting off meeting his parents. Luckily, a sickness kept working its way through her co-workers and his schedule kept him working on Sundays. She'd never feared anything in her life. All that bullshit had been beaten out of her in the lessons that were meant to toughen her up, but only made her angrier, to the point she couldn't function.

At least until she met Gio and he grounded her, made her calm, but he couldn't be around all the time. She still struggled to hold it together from day to day. That's why she didn't want to meet the parents. What if they didn't like her? Gio was close to his family and they were important to him. If they didn't like her would he break up with her?

She also didn't want to admit that she liked her space. He wasn't around all the time so she could do what she wanted. Blast her death metal. Beat the hell out of her heavy bag. She loved her quiet time. She wasn't the clingy sort and Gio loved his job. She knew he did from the way he talked about his days and the people he worked with. They weren't just co-workers but family.

She wasn't one of these women that needed her boyfriend around all the time, but that also didn't mean she didn't like the time she did spend with him. Fuck, they needed to have more sex. Her toys were getting more action than they ever did when she was single. But they weren't Gio. She loved that they weren't all serious and she could be herself. Gio didn't get offended by her sarcasm and her twisted humor.

Sometimes when she did find herself missing him she'd let herself into his place and slept in his bed. When he came home he'd wake her up for work with a kiss and coffee, before passing out.

She was about to kick off her shoes and curl up in bed to watch some horror movie Gio had dropped off for her while she was at work, but the knock on her door made her growl.

Fucking people, showing up without calling.

She threw open the front door, "What the fuck you want?"

"Nice to see you too, baby girl," Gio stood on her stoop smiling down at her. He swooped in and kissed her, she felt his smile against her mouth.

"Shit, I thought you were working." Didn't that sound bitchy?

"No, wanted to surprise you by taking you out. I wrote off for a personal day. We haven't spent enough time together. What do you say? The two of us, dinner, and maybe more later."

"I could do with the more later part."

"I could too, but we're going out. No need to change, you're perfect."

"Sure, I hadn't even thought about food yet."

"Then grab that bag of yours and let's move."

She left him behind and grabbed her battered backpack from the kitchen counter, checked to make sure everything was off and went back to the door.

"Where are we going," She asked as she locked and closed her door.

He took her hand as he led her to his truck.

"It's a surprise."

"I hate surprises."

He laughed as he helped her into the passenger seat. "It's not an ambush. You'll like it so relax."

She did as he said and they talked about their days, he caught her up with the latest firehouse gossip as he drove. They pulled off into a residential area and stopped in front of a large Victorian style house. Flowers hung from baskets along the porch eaves and two rocking chairs sat in front of a huge picture window.

"Where are we?"

"Don't get mad."

"You don't want me mad, that's not the way to start a conversation."

"You're feeling pissy today, I wanted you to meet my parents and because I can't guarantee I'll ever get another Sunday off I thought we'd just show up. It's just the two of them. No crowds."

"What have you done? What if they fucking hate me? What if they think I'm weird? What if—"

Rough hands grabbed her cheeks and she held her breath as he moved in close until their noses almost touched.

"Breathe, baby, you listen to me. They will love you, because you're mine. Okay? As long as their sons are happy with the people they bring home my parents don't judge. They're not like your mom or dad, you've met my brothers, they aren't like yours. I think you're perfect."

"No one is perfect."

"I am, but we're not going to argue. I think you're perfect for me. I want my parents to meet my girlfriend, besides they've heard so much about you they're getting pretty testy that I haven't brought you around yet. Just be you. Don't pretend."

"Being me is a bad idea."

"No, it's not."

Gio tilted his head and pressed his mouth to hers, she closed her eyes as she responded to his firm lips. Her moan was joined by his growl. She found herself pulled across the console and planted on his lap as his hand worked its way up under her skirt. His rough fingers and palm teased the outer curve of her thigh and higher until he pushed beneath her bra. She gasped and arched into his touch, as he pinched her nipple between his fingers.

"Fuck, if we weren't on a street in broad daylight I'd have you on my cock so fast."

She was about to respond when she squeaked as a sharp tapping sound came from the passenger side window. An older version of Gio stared into the window looking way too amused. She pushed Gio's hand from under her dress and attempted to fix her bra cup that was currently under her chin. The hem of her dress had caught on his forearm which meant her lifted dress had her breast exposed. How fucking attractive?

"Son, no sex in front of the house, come inside, you do still have a room."

Her eyes were so wide she felt a twinge as if they were bugged out of their sockets. Gio laughed and hugged her close as she tried to fight to get off of his lap.

"We'll be inside in a minute, Pop, I gotta fix Violet."

"You have five minutes," the man winked then disappeared.

"I'm not going in there. You had your hand up my dress, tit out, man, tit out."

She scrambled off his lap, bra cup still under her chin and she ducked into the floorboard on the passenger seat.

"What the fuck are you doing?"

"Drive, man, drive."

Gio smirked at her, and he chuckled deeply at her growling. She clenched her fists, she'd wipe that look right off his face.

"Fuck, you're cute," Gio opened the door and got out, slammed the door.

She laid her forehead on the warm leather and jumped when the door swung open.

"Get your sexy ass out of the truck now, Violet."

"No," She rumbled louder as she ducked farther under the dash.

"Don't make me do this."

"I'm not making you do shit. I'm going home, whether you like it or not," She made a move toward the driver's seat. "I'll hotwire this bitch and go—"

Gio hands wrapping around her waist had her screeching as she grabbed onto the console.

"Violet, let go."

Her knuckles were white as she dug into the leather.

"Violet Canne, if you don't let go right now, I'm going to spank your ass until you can't sit."

"Fuck you, man, I'll take you out," She tried to kick but he got his arms fully around her waist and dragged her out of the truck. She tried to make herself heavy.

"Violet, I'm not playing with you." His voice was filled with frustration just like the night he told her to turn down her music.

She went completely limp as he too easily carried her toward the house.

"They're going to hate me. Your dad saw my tits. Come on, we'll do it another day."

"Ma, Pop, meet Violet," Gio introduced her as he plopped her down onto her feet. Gio took the underwire of her bra and tugged it down under her breast.

It was either stand or fall into a puddle on the floor, she almost decided to go full *Scarlett O'Hara* vapors. She closed her eyes and took a deep breath, then calmly opened them and looked up at Gio. "I hate you."

"No, you don't, you love me."

"I love you as much as an STD."

The bastard had the nerve to laugh and wink at her, she was going to pluck that offending eye out as soon as they were alone.

"I'm wounded. Now say hello." He spun her around with a smile on his face.

"Did you happen to drop him as a baby?"

He started to rub her upper arms all caring and gentle, she elbowed him in the gut.

"Son, she's so adorable," Gio's mother practically danced on her toes in excitement.

She snarled her nose, tried to ignore the twitch of her eye and turned to look at her soon to be ex-boyfriend, "Sleep light, Gio."

He leaned down and whispered in her ear, "You're so cute."

She hated the way a chill went up her spine and her nipples tightened, pushing against the fabric of her bra. Her life was normal before two months ago—well normal for her and now she had to deal with this shit.

"It's very nice to meet you both."

"We're kind of attached to him, Violet, aim to maim not to kill."

She almost smiled at Gio's dad when he winked at her. She liked the old man.

"Dinner is almost ready to be put on the table. Since it's just the four of us, we're going to eat in the kitchen if that's alright with y'all."

"That's fine."

"Then follow me."

She allowed Gio to nudge her forward to follow his parents. Gio's mom was too perky and light, his dad all smiley and laid-back. She really didn't know how to deal with it. Although, she hid her terror with long practice behind her snark and attitude. It had saved her too many times over the years.

Gio's dad had his hand placed on the base of his wife's back. His fingers caressing Gio's mom through the cotton of her t-shirt. The few times she'd seen her parents interact was one or both of them throwing down wherever they were. The fights were brutal. This shit was almost like walking into some 50's show about the perfect family and that was what made her uneasy. She couldn't do this and that was probably what Gio expected because he'd grown up with it. It was a good thing she didn't mind being single.

"SLEEP LIGHT, GIO" AND LET THE NIGHTMARES BEGIN

*G*io stretched his limbs as he awakened and reached for Violet's side of the bed. She hadn't stayed over with him because she was still pissed about being ambushed about the visit to his parents. He just wanted them to meet his girl. He hadn't expected her to be that upset by it. He hated the cool expanse of the bed beside him. Violet belonged beside him—cuddled up against him.

He sighed heavily and opened his eyes, "What the fuck," he shouted as he found Violet stood beside his bed glaring down at him.

"Good morning, isn't it a lovely day?"

He pushed to a seated position and pressed as far back to the headboard as he could.

"What are you doing?"

"Watching you sleep, all safe in your bed."

He didn't miss the tightening of her tiny fists and her lush lips pulled into a slow, half-smile.

"Violet, I apologized for the ambush."

"No, that's fine, it's all forgotten." She waved her arms in a dismissive manner. "I brought you coffee, it's right there." She pointed at his favorite mug filled with the steaming dark brew.

"Um, did you poison it?"

"Now, Gio, would I do that?"

Her smile was so serene and he'd run into burning buildings, became trapped a time or two, but none of that had made him as fearful as that expression on his girl's beautiful face.

"Aren't you going to drink it, Gio?"

He didn't like the way she said his name. She snarled every time her lips formed the two simple syllables. He was man enough to admit his hands shook a bit as he reached for his mug and he lifted it, brought it to his mouth. Taking a couple sniffs and he watched her from over the rim. He took the smallest sip possible and her grin turned almost evil.

"Dammit, Violet, what did you do," He shouted as he set the mug back down and resisted the urge to spit until the strong coffee taste no longer filled his mouth.

"I didn't do anything. I just thought I'd be nice and fix my sweet boyfriend coffee before I left for work."

"I know better than that," He leaned forward, grabbed her wrist and pulled her onto the bed to straddle his thighs. "I'm sorry, baby, I really am. I just wanted them to meet my beautiful girl."

"I need to be told these things, Gio. I don't do well with—"

He cut her off with a soft kiss and hugged her around the waist. "I promise I'll never surprise you like that again. Now, what did you do to my nectar of life?"

"Nothing, but made you nervous, huh?"

He chuckled as she leaned back and the position thrust her sexy, plump breasts out. He clearly remembered the weight of them in his hands. The texture of her nipples on his tongue— between his teeth. He flexed his arms and pulled her tighter to him. His body craved her. An entire month passed and he missed the taste of her filling his mouth.

"Do you have to go to work?"

"Yes, I do, I have to leave in a few."

"Please come over tonight. I miss you."

He wanted to talk to her. Find out where they stood on their relationship. He'd decided to take Hella's advice but he just didn't know how it was going to go down. The only thing he was certain of was what he wanted—her. He knew Violet liked him. Yet he needed to know if she could come to love him. Did they have a chance for long term?

"I should be home a little after six."

"Dinner will be ready when you get here." He stroked his hands across her lower back to her hips, along the front of her thighs. She shivered as he flipped up the hem of her dress to find her wearing another pair of those sexy, white boy shorts. He traced the seam of her plump pussy lips and his mouth fucking watered. "It's been too long, baby girl."

"It's all yours."

He tucked his fingers under the soft cotton and rubbed her fuzzy lips, her hips rolled and shuddered.

"But not until I get home."

He groaned and threw his head back, "Come on, baby, you know how much I love morning sex."

"I'll spend the night, but I gotta go."

He smiled as he leaned in and tweaked her curls, his mouth brushed hers.

"You sure you can't call in—"

She was whimpering as she pushed off his lap. He felt better when he noticed the hardness of her nipples and the way her hands shook as she smoothed the skirt of her dress. He loved the way she reacted to his touch and closeness. Violet didn't give up control easily. She was strong and independent, he loved those qualities, but she also lost herself at his touch.

"I'm sure. My bills don't pay themselves. And I'm not a candidate for acquiring a Sugar Daddy."

"But, baby girl, I could possibly be persuaded."

She snorted and flipped him off, he was so feeling the love. He'd never met a woman he just felt comfortable with even if she frightened him a bit.

"I have to go, drink your coffee and I hope you get the shits."

"Wow, that's harsh," he said with a smile as she sashayed her sexy self out of his bedroom. He couldn't wait for six o'clock to come around.

* * *

"So, how's things going with your woman," Renz asked.

He had his earpiece in as he tried to put the finishing touches on dinner. Violet didn't like anything too fancy and didn't complain about anything he made. The only thing she required was he made sure she had her chocolate milk. The last time he was at her place that was all he'd seen in her fridge.

"Going good, she's coming over for dinner. She should be here in about half an hour." He opened the oven and slid the lasagna onto the rack. It should be ready by the time she got there. He hoped. He got a little distracted thinking about having his curvy woman for dessert.

"I need your help."

"Anything, what's up?"

"Lyn's birthday is coming up in a few months and I want to do something special for them."

"You always make it special for Lyn. And you stress way too much over a present for your best friend."

"Lyn deserves the best."

He couldn't see how Lyn hadn't noticed Renz's interest yet. They'd been friends since high school. He didn't know if they even realized how they looked to everyone else. The last family dinner, the only way they'd have gotten closer were if Lyn had sat on Renz's lap. They constantly touched. He knew Lyn dated, but as far as he knew Renz hadn't asked anyone out in years.

"You know Lyn loves everything you give them."

"I know, but—"

He frowned as Renz paused and the silence lengthened.

"What's really wrong?"

"Nothing, maybe you can go shopping with me and help."

"We can check our schedules and see what we can do."

"I appreciate it. I'll let you get to preparing for your date."

He didn't like how unsure Renz sounded before the other man disconnected the call. Renz was the middle child and he seemed to get lost in the shuffle of the older louder brothers and the younger spoiled ones. He didn't know what he could do though.

He laughed and shook his head at the shrill quack of Violet's favorite slippers, then the slamming of the front door.

"Gio," she called to him.

"In the kitchen, you're early. I thought I'd have another half hour or so."

"Sorry, shit day, so I skipped out early. I can go home—"

He didn't let her finish as he rushed across the kitchen and wrapped his arms around her. He brought her back to the counter and sat her down beside the sink. He moved to the side to finish washing the few dishes he had left from prepping dinner. When he leaned a bit, and pouted his lips as Violet softly chuckled, she brushed a kiss to his mouth.

"Missed you today."

He was kind of shocked she'd admit it. Violet played her hand pretty close to the vest. That's why he needed this dinner.

"I missed you too. Violet, we need to talk."

"Oh."

Her voice was barely above a whisper and he realized his mistake—how that simple sentence sounded. He pulled his hands from the water and pushed his hips between her thighs. His wet hands rose to cover her cheeks and turn her downcast gaze to his.

"It's not that kinda talk, Violet, I promise. I'm so sorry."

"Then what did you need to talk about?"

"I wanted to apologize for the last month. I've canceled dates. Left in middle of dates. I love my job. It was all I ever wanted to do, but I don't want to lose you because I'm not able—"

"Shut the fuck up."

He felt his eyes widen as he took a step back to look down at her, "What?"

"I'm not clingy, Gio. I wouldn't know how to be. I like my space. I don't need you around twenty-four-seven to know you care. Yeah, I'd like you to throw a little more of that dick my way, but we both got shit to do."

He fought his grin, but he couldn't contain it. The woman never stopped surprising him. "I think my heart just exploded with the overwhelming love I'm feeling right now."

"I'm serious." She pushed at his chest.

He wasn't ready to tell her how serious he was, so he just waited.

"I don't need all that flowery bullshit. Be real. I'm crazy. More than a little hateful. I'm shocked you've stuck around."

"I want this to work, Violet. Like permanent. We're not there yet, but that's what I want. I needed you to know that."

"I'm not going anywhere, shit, I tackled you and you still fell all in lust."

He grabbed her plump ass in his big hands and roughly squeezed the curves. "Oh, the tackling was sexy, but when you pulled up your skirt and showed me this sexy ass. You don't know how much I wanted to fall to my knees and worship it."

"You missed your chance that night, do it now."

The command in her voice hardened his dick until it pushed painfully against the back of his zipper. He took another step back as his eyes took in how she slowly and sensually removed her oversized sleep shirt. She was bare under it except for his favorite boy shorts, this time in pale pink. Nothing got his dick harder than his sexy woman stripping for him. He stayed silent as he watched her shimmy out of her underwear.

She set the heels of her slipper clad feet on the edge of the counter.

"Now, show me what you got."

He wanted to lick every pale stretch mark. Kiss every freckle. He stepped closer and dropped to his knees, her pussy right in his face. He raised his hand and lightly brushed the lush lips and parted them until her swollen clit peaked from between.

He buried his face between her thighs and inhaled the musk of her arousal, he swiped his tongue from the wrinkled skin of her ass to her hard nub. He growled as her taste burst on his tongue and he ate her like a starving man. Sucked and licked, pushed his tongue inside her hot, wet pussy. She tore at his short hair and forced him deeper, held him like he'd get away. That wasn't fucking happening.

His fingers pulled her wider as he nibbled on the more delicate lips, suckled at them. Her cries above him desperate, but he wasn't satisfied. He needed his baby girl to come before he took her.

She cursed, trembled and rode his face like she'd never get enough. He avoided her clit because he didn't think she was giving him enough.

"You want to cum, baby girl, you show me how much you fucking want it." He ordered against her soaked pussy.

Her legs fell over his shoulders, and her thighs took his head in a death hold. She scooted farther to the edge and forced his head deeper.

"I don't think," she groaned, "you want to play with me."

"Oh, baby girl, if there's one thing I want to do, that's play with you." He jerked away from her and surged to his feet. He scooped her up and took her to the table, spreading her out. He watched her flinch a little as the cool surface touched her back.

She was all laid out, her pussy lips glistening and her clit flushed and swollen. He took her hands and placed them on the backs of her thighs, she was held open wide for him. "Don't fucking move."

Her eyes widened and he saw the darkening of her anger mixed with a good amount of lust. He brought his hand flat down on her pussy. The wet slap was loud and obscene, her hips jerked and he loved the sight of her teeth sinking into her lower lip.

No one had ever pushed him as close to the edge as Violet. He prided himself on his calm and control, neither of which he had when it came to Violet. Ruining her for all other men, the only thing he could focus on. He needed her so addicted to his loving that she couldn't think about anyone but him. She wasn't self-conscious as she lay there spread out before him.

He slapped her pussy repeatedly until she was red and swollen, wetness pooled on the table under her curvy ass. He ripped at the front of his jeans as he repeatedly punished her furry lips. He only stopped long enough to ease his zipper down and pushed his jeans down to the middle of his hairy thighs.

His cock was so fucking hard it hurt and jerking with his pulse.

"Fuck me," she growled.

He couldn't wait another second, he positioned his fat cock at her hole and thrust. Her pussy lips hot where they met his groin. He felt the rush of her response as he pushed into her over and over. Wetness poured down over his nuts. Her belly jiggled and her tits bounced with the force of his thrusts. She was so fucking hot and tight around his cock, his dick flexed at the sight of her cream coating his bare shaft.

He slapped his palms down on the table beside her wide hips as she cursed and begged him for harder—faster. Whatever his baby girl wanted. He took her with all his strength with no thought if he was hurting her and she let out these high-pitched grunts every time he bottomed out.

He stopped and her wide panicked eyes met his.

"What the fuck are you—"

He pulled out halfway and began spanking her pretty cunt until she was riding his dick, rolling those beautiful hips. She tore at the gorgeous length of her hair and then she came, wetness splashing between them.

"Shit, little girl, that's sexy, I want one more." He bent over her, the table cutting into the front of his thighs and rode her. His mouth on hers and his tongue licking inside, hers tangling with his. He was going to lose it any minute, but he needed one more from her. Their bodies were pressed together and he felt the painful clench of her around him. The cut of her nails into his back and he took her long, agonized groan.

"Where you want it, baby, you," he snapped his hips forward, ground against her, "want me to pull out."

"Don't you fucking dare," she growled then her teeth took his bottom lip.

His balls drew up tight as he pushed through the pleasure swollen, velvet of her pussy. Her whines tinged with pain pushed him over and he sealed his hips against her ass. His eyes rolled back as he spilled every drop inside her. He kissed her lazily as he rocked his hips drawing out their pleasure.

"Keep doing that shit, and I'm yours forever."

"That was the fucking plan."

They collapsed on the table, exhausted and covered in sweat. He'd never been fucking happier in his life and she wasn't going a fucking place.

SHIT, IS THIS WANT HAPPILY EVER AFTER FELT LIKE?

*V*iolet could barely move, putting on her underwear that morning had been a nightmare. Gio had showed no mercy and she hadn't asked for any. The man always seemed so in control. For a minute in the kitchen she'd been shocked by her boldness. She could fake confidence with the best of them, but she wasn't as comfortable with her curves. Don't get her wrong, she didn't mind them, but she was fine with average men —ones who weren't rocking eight ridges of muscle like some freak of nature.

He made her feel sexy and she couldn't deny he wanted her. She'd awakened that morning with him already buried deep and loving her slow and easy. He never seemed satisfied until she got off at least twice. He'd given her breakfast in bed and then he walked her over to her place. When he'd kissed her she hadn't want to go inside without him, but he said he needed to get to work.

Gio wanted permanent—with her. She had to wonder about the man's sanity. Finally it was lunchtime and she was sitting in the break room having her lunch leftovers from dinner last night.

"Violet, you have a visitor," Heather, the receptionist, peeked into the room.

She couldn't stand the bitch. She had one of those better than attitudes because Heather had zero body fat and a rich boyfriend. Women should be self-sufficient—able to handle their own shit.

"Yeah, who is it," She asked as she looked longingly at her food.

"He claims to be your boyfriend."

"Ain't no claim about it," Gio sounded irritated as he walked into the room. "Hey, baby girl."

"What are you doing here?"

"I was hoping to grab you for lunch, but it looks like you already started."

"You can join me."

He hummed and that sexy smirk pulled at one corner of his mouth, "Wasn't exactly what I had in mind to eat."

She snorted as Heather turned and left, she swore the woman muttered *she never* under her breath. He let out a booming laugh as he approached and kissed her before he sprawled onto a chair beside her.

"A little uptight, ain't she?"

"Rich boyfriend, I think he's old enough to be her father. Maybe he ain't giving her the dick like he should."

"Happy you don't have that problem?"

"Looking for compliments?"

"Not in the least. Ma called and asked would we come out Sunday for dinner. I already arranged for the day off. My brother Gibson is visiting."

"Where does he live?"

"Not far away, but he took over as Chief for a small station in some town called Powers. He loves it there and he likes being the boss."

"I guess I could be persuaded to attend, since you're not surprising me this time."

"How many times to I have to apologize?"

"I think your fear over me poisoning your coffee was enough."

He bowed his head as he leaned forward, then rested his forearms on his knees. "So glad my fear is such a turn-on for you."

"We all have our things," she whispered as she leaned in and gently brushed her lips to his.

"You okay today?"

"I'm fine. To be honest, I'm enjoying the reminders."

She loved the way he smiled at her and the corners of his eyes crinkled. Up close she started to notice fine threads of silver in his thick hair. She hummed, "I think I'm dating my own old man," she raised her hand and traced the pale, shimmering hairs.

"Too old for you?"

"No, I think just about right."

"Stay over at my place tonight, I don't like when you're not in my bed."

Her stomach flipped at his softly spoken order. "I think I can do that."

She didn't know what was happening to her. She didn't mind being away from him. She was used to her own space, but she had noticed this strange feeling of actually missing him when they were apart. Even if they couldn't be together at night she loved their conversations. The time Gio spent working didn't mean they hadn't spent a lot of time getting to know each other.

A day never passed where they didn't speak or sneak in a few minutes for a cuddle. She hadn't realized how starved she was for someone to want her with all her unattractive quirks.

"Hey, what's the frown for," Gio asked as he drew her onto his lap.

"It's just weird that you like me."

"I more than like you, Violet, I did talk about us working toward permanent."

She wrapped her arms around his neck and buried her face

against his neck. "I know, but I'm not used to all this shit. Two months ago I was—"

"Just remember, I don't want to change you, baby girl. I think you're perfect as is. I love your attitude. Your curves. The way you don't take my shit. I truly believe you were made for me."

"I think you might be crazier than I am."

"Possibly."

She nipped at his throat and he groaned, tightening his arms around her.

"I may be late getting home tonight, but I wanted to drop this off."

She held on as he leaned back to dig in his pocket. He pulled something out and then opened his hand, a key rested on his palm.

"I had this made before I came to see you. I wanted to drop it off so you can come and go as you please."

"I've never gotten a key before."

"Well, I'd like my girl to start staying over at my place and not have to pick the lock to get in."

She picked the key up and felt the warm metal between her fingertips.

"We all have our talents, Gio, some of mine just aren't exactly legal."

"And I love them all. So, be waiting at my place when I get home?"

"With my ducky slippers on."

He growled as he kissed her, "Those fucking slippers are sexy as fuck especially when that's all you're wearing."

"I think you might be a pervert."

"But I'm your pervert, so be in bed with the slippers on. I have plans for you."

"I look forward to them."

He leaned in close to her ear, "You got any plugs in that toy box of yours?"

"I may." She laughed as his guttural rumble.

His phone pinged in his pocket, "Dammit, breaks over. I'll see you tonight."

He kissed her hard, lingered before he seemed to force himself away from her. He gently eased her off his lap and back into her chair.

She didn't care what she looked like as she watched his ass as he swaggered out of the room. She snarled as Heather stuck her head back in the room.

"He's your boyfriend?"

"Yeah, what of it?"

"Nothing, nothing," the woman visibly swallowed and disappeared.

She picked at the now barely warm lasagna as she stared at the key that rested in front of her. Was shit going too fast? Everything seemed so right when she was in Gio's arms. He spoke of wanting her in his life for the long-term. Gave her a key to his place. Loved what everyone else seemed to find abhorrent about her. She liked that she didn't have to pretend she was something she wasn't to make Gio happy.

He cared for her, but he also wanted to fuck her, that was a nice bonus. Because that man hit every one of her trigger buttons and some she didn't even know she had.

Part of her hoped she was enough. She wasn't delusional enough to think her past didn't shape a lot of her habits. She'd always had to be the toughest. Crying was a weakness. She could throw down with men three times her size. All those things had been points of pride for her until she realized they had shaped her into something she didn't really want to be. She loved her strength and her attitude, but that didn't mean she wouldn't like someone to take care of her—like Gio did.

She just hoped she didn't ruin it. She might not be ready to admit it to him, but she was falling in love—or what she thought love should feel like.

HIS FAMILY LOVED HER

$\mathcal{H}$e stood beside Renz as the man stared at the glass encased jewelry. The man was chewing his thumb nail until it looked raw. "Dude, fucking stop, Lyn will love whatever you get."

"I know, I know, but—"

"Renz, why don't you tell Lyn how you feel," he asked. Everyone else danced around the issue. Didn't want to push it because Renz was sometimes insecure. He was a little chunkier than the rest of them. Well, he carried a bit more weight about his middle like their dad.

"I don't want to lose Lyn. Can you imagine? Twenty years of friendship and I go up to Lyn to tell them I've loved them since high school. I can't be without Lyn. Lyn has been there through all the bullshit and never once judged me for being awkward or my terrible sense of humor."

"Then why don't you just tell them?"

"I can't, man, it kills me to watch Lyn go out on dates, but it would hurt more if Lyn didn't want to have anything to do with me. Lyn thinks I'm straight. I love Lyn whether they're feeling their suits or jeans and t-shirts, or when they put on their prettiest dress. Everything about Lyn just does it for me."

He didn't want to push too much. Renz had a tendency to shut down when he felt threatened. No one would judge Renz for his love for his best friend. They'd be happy that Renz found his person.

"What about Violet? We all love her. When are you going to make that shit official?"

"I don't know about that, man. We've been together three months—"

"Practically living together."

"Not living together. She just stays over and I love when she's there when I get home, whether she's asleep or not."

Okay, she spent more time at his place, but it wasn't like they minded all that much. He loved her stuff next to his on the bathroom counter. Her pretty dresses hung up in his closet. Okay, they were living together. He smiled to himself as he left Renz to look at lockets. Renz had already picked out an expensive watch for Lyn to wear to the office and his brother wanted to get something beautiful for Lyn to wear when they went out.

He turned to study his brother for a minute and saw the man checking out rings, there was a deep sadness that made the faint lines on Renz's face deeper. At thirty-five, Renz was exactly in the middle. Ma and Pop had their youngest five back to back, nearly a year apart that included a set of twins. Catholics and their birth control was sin policy. Ma and Pop never complained, they'd both come from big families and they'd wanted one themselves. But with so many Renz kind of got lost. Renz learned to take care of himself and the siblings below him.

Lyn was the only person he'd ever been selfish over. Renz didn't hide his affection. Showed Lyn in every way that Renz loved Lyn, but never in the romantic way. The way Renz really wanted to love on them.

He felt bad. He'd seen the envious expression aimed at Tony

and Esther when they went off to make out, laughed softly about something. He'd noticed it a few times aimed in his and Violet's direction. He shook his head and looked in the cases as he passed.

A simple platinum band with a rose carved pink stone caught his attention.

"Did you see something you like, sir," an older saleslady strolled up to him.

"Yes, could I look at that one, please?" He pointed it out and waited as the lady removed it. He held it between his big fingers.

An image of Violet wearing it flashed in his mind. Snug on her ring finger and he smiled, as he stroked the surface of the rose.

"Rose quartz."

"My girlfriend loves pink."

"If you're looking for engagements rings, I can show you some more appropriate options."

"No, she'd love this one."

He'd studied the way their fingers laced together so many times he knew her delicate ring finger was just a little slimmer than his pinkie. He slid it on and it caught at his knuckle.

"I want this."

"I'll put it in a box, was there anything else you'd like to see?"

"No, just this." He reluctantly handed it back to her and followed her toward the register. He didn't think twice when he handed over his card.

He knew three months wasn't a long time, well, it had been four since she'd tackled him in their front yard. But that didn't mean he didn't know it was right. It may not be time yet. When he felt the moment was right he'd be prepared. He's known almost from the beginning that Violet was it for him. He loved her. He hadn't said it yet, neither had she.

She still held a part of herself back and he didn't know why. He took his card and the small bag holding the black jeweler's box.

"You got something for Violet?"

"Yes. What about you? Find something for Lyn?"

"Yeah, they're going to wrap it up for me. Do you want to grab a beer before you head home?"

"Sure, Violet's got some charity function. They needed two people for crowd control. I never realized what a nightmare being an event planner was. No wonder my baby girl is crazy."

"Wouldn't have her any other way, right?"

"Hell no, she's fucking perfect."

"Must be love, I'll just pay for my stuff and meet you out front."

"Deal." He walked away to leave Renz with some privacy. Even though he was curious about Lyn's gift he didn't want to ask just in case it was private. His phone ringing in his pocket pulled him from his thoughts and he removed it, connected the call as he pressed it to his ear.

"Masiello."

"Hey, are you home yet," Violet's voice was almost drowned out by the noise in the background.

"No, I'm out with Renz, did you need something?"

"No, some drunk got handsy—"

He growled and she giggled.

"Man, don't even, do you think I can't take care of myself?"

"That's not the point, Violet, you're mine, remember, mine?"

"All yours, big guy. Okay, we have to have a sewing kit around here somewhere. Thin ass straps are not big tit friendly."

"Those are my—"

"Possessive, aren't we?"

"You know it, how much longer you playing referee?"

"Actually, I shouldn't be but another hour, two at the most. It's sort of winding down. I think Irene will be good to handle everything after the auction ends. Did Renz decide on a present for Lyn yet? He's been looking for like two months?"

"He found something."

"What he get," she demanded.

He snorted at her excitement. "I don't know, he kinda wanted me to leave him alone while he paid."

"It better have been a goddamn engagement ring. He's fucking around way too much."

"You want to tell him that? I'll give him the phone."

"No, I got his number," and with that the call disconnected.

What the fuck, his woman just hung up on him.

"Dude, did you sic your old lady on me," Renz growled as he held the phone away from his ear as he exited the store. "No, I didn't get a damn engagement ring. Are you insane? Yeah, yeah, I know stupid question."

He attempted to wipe his smile away as Renz argued with Violet. She fit in so easily. His parents adored her. His brothers loved her but were slightly frightened. But he did noticed Violet had a bit of soft spot for Renz and Niccolo.

Renz growled and shoved his phone into his pocket.

He jumped as his phone rang and when he answered his woman was pissed.

"Did that motherfucker hang up on me? Tell him imma kick his ass next time I see him."

Then she proceeded to disconnect the call on him. When had his life spiraled out of control?

"She said she's going to kick your ass next time she sees you."

"She's very violent, are you sure you want to make all that permanent?"

"Damn right, I got the ring to prove it." He announced as he walked to his truck and walked around to the driver's side.

"Shit, man, you didn't tell me, when are you going to ask?"

He didn't answer until they were headed in the direction of their favorite pub. A lot of firefighters and cops went there to unwind. Maybe they'd catch a few of their brothers there as well. "I don't know, she's not ready yet and I'm more than happy to keep things as is."

"I'm happy for you. I might bitch, but she's perfect for you."

"I think so too."

They lapsed into silence, but it wasn't uncomfortable. They'd spent their whole lives together. He could tell just from looking at one of his brothers what the man was feeling or thinking. Renz had some shit to work through in his head. Even as he was excited about his and Violet's future, he knew Renz was nowhere near as confident as to what the years ahead of him held.

VIOLET WAS GOING TO JAIL

*S*he pulled into her driveway close to midnight. Pissed that she'd told Gio she'd be home hours ago but like with his job what they planned wasn't always what happened. She narrowed her eyes as a massive shadow stepped off her porch. Once the figure was close enough to catch in her headlights she felt the rage prickling beneath her skin.

Motherfucker, knew better, she reached into the back and pulled the wooden bat from the floorboard. She kicked off her high heels and jumped out of her car. Ronald Canne stood in front of her car with his thick arms crossed over his chest. His belly rounder than the last time she saw him.

"I know you better have a damn good excuse for being on my doorstep." She pointed the bat in his direction.

"Now, is that any way to greet your father, half-pint?"

"My so-called father would know I'd beat his ass down on my lawn if he showed up without calling."

"Lettie, I need a place to crash."

She snarled at the use of the stupid nickname.

"Plenty of shelters around, fucking find one."

He moved closer and she took the bat in both hands, not too tight just enough of a grip to get a nice arc on it.

"Need to find my daughter-in-law, she knew how a man needed to be treated."

"You ain't finding her, old man, I made sure none of y'all could get your hands on her, especially Clem." There was no way she'd let them anywhere near Peggy. Peggy had been so beaten down by the time she'd helped the woman escape Peggy barely knew if she could use the bathroom without asking permission. Peggy wouldn't even look her in the eyes for fear of getting hit. That wasn't going to happen again on her watch. "You want to get off my property in one piece or I'll kneecap you and drag you to the curb."

"You think you have it in you? Think you can take me and him," Ronald pointed to her left and another mass stepped out of the darkness.

"We ain't been around to keep you tough. Got soft, girl," Clem spoke from where he stood about six feet from her.

Fucking great, she rolled her eyes.

Clem looked her up and down in her silky dress and she knew what he saw when he looked at her. Women were useless outside the bedroom or taking care of the men. It was one of the reasons she'd fought them so hard growing up. She'd even worked to be tougher than her mom who she knew had a body count to go along with her vicious reputation.

SHE'D TAKEN on all four of her brothers at once and walked away, two on one were way better odds. She took a step back.

Rule one: keep them off her back.

They liked to go for the throat. She darted a glance at Gio's and saw all the lights were off. On her own, at least the odds were in her favor.

Ronald lunged in her direction and she ran around the back

of her car. The empty yard to her back. She swung the bat, it came across the side of Ronald's left knee. He went down with a shout, but she'd been too distracted by him. Clem's thick arms came around her, trapping hers against her chest and she threw her head back, connected with his nose. She felt a sense of satisfaction when she heard the crunch and knew she'd broken it.

"What the fuck is going on here," Gio's voice boomed. "You better put her down right now."

Clem surprisingly did what was ordered and she slammed the end of the bat into his gut, bending him in half. She turned to find Gio, Renz, Sal, and Montes seething in the porch light.

"Why are you having a brawl on our front lawn?"

"What brawl," She asked sweetly and elbowed her oldest brother in the face, listening to the satisfying crunch.

"Violet," He shouted her name sharply

Oh, how she loved that tone of his voice. It meant rage sex. She loved rage sex.

"This bitch tried to kneecap me," Ronald complained from the ground.

"Violet, please, come here."

"Yes, Gio," She answered sweetly and as she passed her father she kicked the fucker in the face.

"Violet."

"I don't know why you yell at her, Gio, your girl does whatever the fuck she wants."

She snorted at Sal as the man rolled his eyes, then the big man winked at her.

"Now, explain."

"Ronald, male contributor to my DNA thought he'd crash at my place. Sibling thought he'd probably get his punching bag of an ex-wife back. Two against one are a lot better odds than I had as a kid. Normally all four of my brothers stomped me into the ground."

There was an echoing of deep, dangerous rumbles coming

from Gio and his brothers. "Oh shit, I took care of it. See, they're down. No need to get in trouble." They all loved their jobs. No way in hell she would ruin something they'd wanted to do their entire lives.

Montes spoke up, "They did get their asses kicked by a cute little munchkin."

"Fuck you, man, I'm short but I'm vicious."

"Renz, take Violet inside while we take care of the trash."

"Aw, Gio, come on, I was looking forward to taking the trash broken and bloody to the curb."

"You'll go inside and get comfortable, you had a late night."

She couldn't believe she was agreeing after he hugged her to his side, kissed the top of her head. "Fine, I'm keeping my bat though."

"I wouldn't even dream of taking it away. You did look awful sexy using that damn thing."

"You watched?"

"As much as I wanted to step in, I trust you to protect yourself, and I had a feeling about who they were. If I thought for a second they'd hurt you in anyway—"

"Thanks for letting me handle it."

She loved that he let her take care of her own shit. He didn't try to step in and take over. If she wanted to be alone at her place he gave her the space she needed. Same with him, if he wanted to go out with his brothers and friends she never stopped him. They were dating, they weren't each other's parole officers.

"Violet, you were taking care of yourself a helluva lot longer than I've been around. I love you and trust you to know what you can and can't handle."

She leaned into his side and stroked her fingertips down his cotton covered abs, lower until they danced over the fly of his jeans.

"You're awful sexy when you let me kick some ass. I'll reward you later."

All the brothers snorted and she let Renz take her inside.

"That fucking bitch, she won't always have you watching her fat—"

"You're talking about my future wife and their future sister-in-law, you really want to take us on, old man. Especially after you already got your ass kicked by my baby girl?"

She felt that strange heating of her cheeks again and she couldn't help the big smile that stretched her lips.

"He must really like me," She looked up at a smiling Renz.

"You could say that, Violet."

"No one has ever liked me before."

"Too bad, because we all love you. You're family."

"I've never had one of those either."

"Go on upstairs and take a shower, get into your comfortable clothes. Your man will want to make sure you're all right when he comes in."

She nodded and really didn't know how to respond. She'd been alone most of her life. Barely tolerated. She walked upstairs to Gio's, well, their bedroom. It had been hers for the last month. Everything at her place was pretty much moved over since all she owned were her clothes and her sex toys. Even some of those had made it to Gio's place.

Entering the bathroom, she didn't bother turning on the lights. A nightlight glowed over the sink, she turned on the shower and stripped. She let out a long sigh as she stepped beneath the scalding water. Her thoughts turned chaotic and for the first time in months the doubts assailed her with what ifs. She knew Gio wanted her. Told her plenty of times, but would that still be the case months down the road—years? It didn't help the secret she was keeping from him. She hadn't been scared about much, if anything in her life, but what she needed to tell him would probably end them.

She scrubbed herself down and then stepped out of the stall, she dried herself hearing Gio and his brothers talking downstairs. She did owe her knight in turnout gear a reward. She grinned to herself as she went to prepare. If all she got was one more night she was going to make sure she made the best of it.

WOULD SHE SAY YES?

$\mathcal{H}$e pushed his bitching brothers out the door, they'd spent the last hour making a nuisance of themselves and delaying his evening with his woman. He had taken a sick day because he had plans for his vicious little woman and he wasn't letting her out of bed. That was after she said yes. He reached into the pocket of his plaid, cotton shirt and after making sure everything was locked up and turned off he headed upstairs. He hoped Violet hadn't fallen asleep.

The door was open and the electric candles burned inside his bedroom. He stopped in the doorway and froze at the sight that greeted him. Violet was sprawled across his bed, naked except for those yellow ducky slippers and she worked a vibrator over her beautiful pussy. Sweat misted her skin and shimmered under the candlelight. She arched and whimpered. His swallowed hard as his cock jerked.

"Baby girl, you started without me," he approached the bed, unbuttoning his shirt and slipped it off, then carefully laid it across the foot of the bed.

"I had to get all nice and ready for you," her voice was low and husky.

When she parted her legs farther and tossed her toy aside, he saw the flared base of a dark pink plug.

"Oh, now, that, baby girl, is what I love to see."

He didn't remove his jeans, he needed some protection against his girl. She knew exactly how to break him to make him lose control. They rarely went a day without sex or teasing, he'd found he loved extended foreplay. Finding all the ways that took her breath or elicited those sexy sighs.

He crawled up the bed, kissing the silkiness of her skin with the fine, pale hairs. He loved his girl natural and couldn't get enough of her. He alternated licking along her inner thighs until they quivered under his lips. He couldn't wait any longer and he buried his face between her soaked lips.

He gripped the base of the plug, pulled and pushed it out of her tight little ass. The vision of her plumping her breasts, she tugged and twisted her nipples made him reach for his dick. Palming the thick length and grunted at the pleasure. He kissed his way up the rounded softness of her belly.

"Baby girl, you want me," he asked.

She only nodded and moaned, he reached for his shirt. It was a dirty trick but he didn't give a fuck. He searched until he took the cool circle of metal between his fingers.

"Now, if you want me to pound that ass of yours, you have to answer a question."

"Whatever it is, yes."

The desperation in her voice made him smile and he tapped at her plug. His baby girl did love her ass played with, but they'd never gotten to the anal. He'd never been able to resist her pussy long enough.

"Now, now, baby girl, that's not how it works. You need to focus."

"I have a plug in my ass and I've been using my vibrator for ten minutes and you think I'm going to fucking focus. Don't make me take it."

He chuckled and then found himself on his back, she was working his pants undone with hurried motions.

He held the ring in front of her face and she froze.

"What the fuck is that?"

"Permanence."

"You want to marry me—me? Are you—"

"I love you, I've been holding onto this ring for a month, waiting for the right time. I want you to be mine, today, tomorrow, years from now."

Then she jerked away and she looked pissed, where the hell had he fucked up?

"You found the fucking test, didn't you? I don't need you to fucking marry me just because you knocked me up."

His brain went blank, "What the fuck are you talking about?"

"Oh shit, nothing, I have to go."

He grabbed her hips before she could escape. Out of all the time he'd known Violet, he'd never seen her afraid and her features were etched with terror. He never wanted to see that look again.

"Violet, talk to me…now."

"Um, I took a test last month."

"And?"

"It was positive."

He'd never been fucking harder, he took his cock out, shoved the denim down his thighs, and he lifted her hips enough to ease into her. The plug made her tighter. He noticed things he hadn't before. Her sexy stomach was rounder. Her upper body bowed and drove her down harder on his dick.

"You're going to say yes. You're going to marry me. I'm going to fuck you whenever and wherever I want."

"Is that right?"

"You'll do as I say."

"Maybe I don't wanna."

Even as she denied it she started to ride his cock, lifted her gorgeous body up and down. He couldn't take his gaze off the sensual motions of her curvy form. She arched and trembled, whimpered as she threw her head back. Her long hair tickled his upper thighs. It was as far as he'd gotten his pants down.

"Why do I always end up still dressed when I'm inside you?"

"You have no fucking control."

He rolled her to her back and her thighs tightly gripped his sides. He took her slow and easy, he wanted to love on her. He kissed her between whispered words of love and praise. Told and showed her how much he loved her, wanted her to always be his. He'd never forgotten protection in his fucking life but with her it had never crossed his mind.

"Tell me you love me, Violet."

He needed to hear the words. It didn't matter if he knew she did he needed to hear them.

"I love you."

He fucked into her in slow, long strokes. "Say it again."

"I love you," she said the words softly, then her teeth sunk into her lower lip.

"Do you want to be fucked, baby girl?"

"Yes, please."

He'd never make his baby girl beg. He eased out of her and turned her until he braced herself on her hands and knees.

"I want you to grab your toy and press it to your clit," He ordered as he eased the plug out. He spotted the lube and slicked himself to make sure he didn't hurt his baby girl. Taking his cock in hand he pressed to her stretched ass and pushed in just as he heard the buzz of her toy. He laid his chest to her back and laced the fingers of his right through hers.

He pounded into her as he lowered his head to press his lips to her ear.

"I love everything about you." He took her rougher and quicker. "Fucking perfection." He bit at her shoulder, sucked until he knew he left a mark. He was going to lose it too quick. She teased his nuts with the vibrator and he sealed his hips to her ass, grinding against her. Her tortured scream was all it took before he came inside her. She was fucking herself on his cock, slamming her ass back against him. She knew he wasn't happy if she didn't release for him at least twice.

"That's right," His throat was tight, "Give me one more." He let his girl use him because he'd give her anything she wanted. He licked the salt of her sweat from her neck as she tightened around him until he knew his eyes fucking crossed. He collapsed to the side, both of them moaning as the loss of contact. He didn't want his full weight on his girl.

She was spread out on her stomach, her damp hair covering her face and he smiled as he turned her to shut off her toy. He found the ring in the tangled sheets and took her left hand. He stared into her heavy-lidded eyes as he slid it onto her finger.

"You're not mad?"

"Baby girl, there's a lot I can be mad about," He stroked her stomach, "This will never be one of them. Not exactly planned, but a really great surprise." He leaned in to gently kiss her lips. "I want a girl."

"Why?"

"So, she can be as badass as you."

He savored her tiny giggle that sounded so carefree. Different from the woman he'd met the night she'd taken him out in their front yard. He may not have seen this happening, but there's nothing he regretted about making her his. He stroked his fingertips down the indent of her spine and felt her shiver. "You ready for round two?"

"Always."

He slipped off the bed, took her in his arms and carried her to the bathroom, he held her as he turned on the shower. Stepped under the quickly warming water. He carefully set her on her feet and fell to his knees in front of her.

"I already put the ring on your finger, but, Violet, will you marry me?"

"I don't know. Your job sucks. You like to boss me around—"

"I dare you."

"Now, Gio, why didn't you just say so?"

EPILOGUE

NO SHOTGUN WEDDING

"Holy shit, did her water just break," Renz yelled in the back of the limo.

"Calm down, it's completely natural. Fucking men," Violet growled as she placed her hands on the contracted curve of Lauren's stomach. "How long?"

"I thought I could make it."

Her best friend sounded miserable and she wasn't having the easiest time moving around in the cramped space of the limo with her own swollen stomach. The twins were being assholes today.

"We're going to the hospital," she heard Gio telling the driver.

She noticed her husband to be on the phone and rearranging everything. He knew she wasn't going to do anything but be by Lauren's side. They'd gone to every birthing class with Lauren. Memorized every detail of Lauren's birthing plan.

"Lauren, why didn't you tell us," Gio asked as he moved behind her friend and rubbed her belly in slow circles.

She smiled at them, Gio knew every one of Lauren's cravings. The man might as well have two pregnant girlfriends, he just didn't fuck one of them.

"You're going to miss your wedding because of me."

"Shut up, Lauren."

"Listen to Violet, I called the priest and he's coming to the hospital. We're still getting married and Violet is going to have her best friend at her side. It's going to be perfect."

She loved the man more than she could ever say and he felt the same, embraced her endless irritation and moods. Didn't even mind when she woke up horny in the middle of the night and hopped on his thick cock before the man's eyes even opened. A woman had needs and apparently a pregnant one had a lot.

It was chaos once they arrived at the emergency room. Gio's parents descended along with Maximo, Tony and Sal. Sal had attended classes when Gio couldn't. He was the backup birthing coach. Niccolo and Montes stayed behind to take everyone over to the reception and was working crowd control. She felt bad they'd miss the ceremony.

Lauren was complaining and worried about ruining the wedding. Her best friend had been there. Never left her side even when Violet had worked her ass off to push the other woman away. No way would she miss out on her niece being born. Lauren was admitted and moved to a room.

"Who's getting married, we might be in a bit of a hurry here?"

The priest's face brightened with a huge smile as he breezed into the room.

"Me and Violet, our niece couldn't wait to be born."

"I see that, so, do we have everything, rings and all?"

Everyone nodded.

"Then let's get the show on the road. It doesn't look like we have much time."

Violet looked up at Gio and he smiled down at her as they listened to the Priest begin. There was a lot she'd never expected from life and this big, loving man was one of them. Her face heated as he mouthed *I love you* and they said their I dos just as a scream made her cringe. They shared a quick kiss before they turned in time to catch Sal keeping eye contact with Lauren.

This wasn't the life she'd planned, but no way in fuck would she regret a second, especially not taking out the sexy firefighter next door.

THE END

ABOUT THE AUTHOR

J.M. Dabney is a multi-genre author who writes mainly LGBT romance and fiction. She lives with a constant diverse cast of characters in her head. No matter their size, shape, race, etc. she lives for one purpose alone, and that's to make sure she does them justice and give them the happily ever after they deserve. J.M. is dysfunction at its finest and she makes sure her characters are a beautiful kaleidoscope of crazy. There is nothing more she wants from telling her stories than to show that no matter the package the characters come in or the damage their pasts have done, that love is love. That normal is never normal and sometimes the so-called broken can still be amazing.

Trenton Security

Livingston

Little

Masiello Brothers

The Taming of Violet

3 Moments Trilogy

A Matter of Time